Tiffany Passmore

Tiffany Passmore   Iris

The Garden 2
Iris

Praise for Orchid:

I enjoyed reading this book. It is very descriptive and allows your imagination to soar. ☐ 5 of 5 Stars! ~ Christina Walton-Lewis

(Author of Love Letters, Becoming Ready To Be Loved)

"A story to pull you in from the beginning. From innocence to awakening, watch it all unfold in the beautiful rooms named after flowers. Graphic while attentive to subtle details. This book will get you hooked on the series... Perfect for a night a home--get your goodies and snuggle up to Orchid!" 5 of 5 Stars! ~ Kira Takenouchi

(Bestselling Author of Headmaster's Chambers, Taming Riki and Once A Chieftain)

Tiffany Passmore   Iris

In Japan, the Japanese Penal Code sets a minimal age of consent of 13 regardless of gender or sexual orientation. However, the Children Welfare Act chapter 34 forbids any act of "fornication" (淫行) with children (here defined as anyone under 18 years of age) with prefectures and districts specifying further details in (largely similar) "obscenity ordinances" (淫行条例) **like adding exemptions for sex in the context of a sincere romantic relationship (typically determined by parental approval).**
Wikipedia, 2018

The Garden Book 2

IRIS

Iris, The Garden series book 2 is a work of fiction. Names, characters, places, and incidents either are the product of the author's imagination or are used fictionally. Any resemblance to actual persons, living or dead, events, or locales is entirely coincidental.

Chapter 1

The locker room held the gaiety of youth as the soccer team bounded inside. Harsh breathing and sweat seemed to be the unanimous condition of each teenager. "Boys, boys," The chuckle in the coaches voice testimony to his love of not only the sport but the team as well. He stood in his polo shirt the same white uniform he wore everyday at their practice. Kiyoko, his lovely wife kept it free of stains.

Coach Tanaka brushed his silver hair back over his forehead. The few wrinkles there testimony to his long days in the sun. His deep set, double lidded eyes squinted against the bright light in the locker room.

Dull silver shone along the polished white walls from the lockers full of the various sundry of the team. "Great practice today. I am sure, as long as we play like we usually do, tomorrows game is ours." Coach Tanaka stood for a moment as the room emptied of the rambunctious youth. The din of their banter dying down. The setting sun cast bright rays illuminating the name plates of the lockers.

Tanaka's eyes fell on the lockers of his two most prominent players, Kenji and Kouji Mochizuki. The boys had singular talent having pushed the team to the finals. He was sure that it was only a matter of time before professional teams were looking at their talent. They had one advantage over the other team mates; their parents made it to every game. Sometimes they were in business suits or running late, but they made it.

"Hey, Ni-Ji" Coach Tanaka chuckled as Ichigani, another top player referred to the twins by the name that they had come up with when no one could tell them apart. Aside from their eye color, there was not a notable difference. While their dad was a prominent Japanese business man owning one of the biggest shipping companies in the area, their mother was a Korean, American mix with startling green eyes that she has passed to her sons. Both boys also had her hair color. The color of warm honey. "Your parents are here." Ichigani grinned pointing to the door of the locker room. His own wild ravens black locks released from his hair tie. He looked down at the two boys grinning as he smiled at them.

    Coach Tanaka waved the other boys off , "Hit the showers the rest of you. We don't want Mochizuki sama to faint at the smell of you." Coach Tanaka smiled at the lovely lady that had married his dear friend. Her lineage was not the best pedigree of Japanese heritage that his own family admired yet her smile could light up a room.

Kenji and Kouji dashed to the door with a large smile on their face. Kouji paused as he approached his parents. Something in the way that his mother clung to his father. Her grip on his sleeve leaving her hands lacking in blood. Her eyes rimmed in red, glistening. With shaking hands, she reached for her sons. " Ken Chan, Kou Chan," Kenji gasped feeling her cold hand as it brushed his face. His mother had always been warm. Her hand stroked his face as it always had. He closed his eyes turning his face into her palm which smelled of lilies and white roses. Her signature scent. Mrs Mochizuki sniffled, "We have terrible news."

Kouji placed a hand on Kenji as his brother paled. He always had been perceptive. Seeing his mother so drawn, his father's tight lipped stance Kenji knew that he would not like whatever they had come to practice to tell them. He could only think of one reason. "It's grandpa, isn't it?" He asked almost afraid of the answer even as he knew it. Last winter a bout of pneumonia had almost taken their grandfathers life and he was never quite the same.

Usually every Christmas Grampy came to Osaka to visit them, last year, he had not been able to. Kouji firmed his spine as his father nodded. "No..." Kenji gasped his lips turned down into a poked out lower while his eyes filled. He looked up at his brother not realizing that he had sat on the metal bench off the wall.

Mr Mochizuki heaved a sigh. He placed a hand on Kouji's shoulder feeling the tremble. He pulled him into an embrace. After a moment he stepped back, "Your mother and I are going to Korea this Sunday. You boys behave yourself while we are gone. We have Okumara-San from next door to look in on you over the time that we are gone. If he doesn't make it we will send for you." Kouji nodded as Kenji wiped his face. He pulled his mother into his arms feeling her slight frame tremble as she wept.

"Will grampy make it?" Kouji asked as his brother comforted their mother. Their father smiled at him. Kouji felt his own eyes begin to glisten. He knew that smile. That sad, watery smile he gave when he knew that he could not tell his family what they wanted to hear so he said nothing at all. Kouji looked away from his father in his dark suit. His father always wore a dark suit.

Growing up, Kouji had thought he wore the same suit every day. It was not until he was older that he noted his parents dressing room where there was a wide assortment of dark suites with accessories. The watched gleamed in the light next to the cuff links and tie pins. He vowed then to become a business man just like him.

"It was a stroke, that lead into a heart attack. He is in a coma." Mrs Mochizuki sniffled accepting the handkerchief that her husband handed her. She dabbed at her eyes. "After mother passed on, he just doesn't have it in him anymore to fight. When we go to Korea, if he is not awake we have to tell them to take him off the machines as was his wish." She crumpled then laying her head on Kenji's chest allowing her son to support her as they sat on the cool metal bench warming under them.

"Oh... Grampy," Kenji whispered. "Please wake up." The coach sighed as the distraught family left his gym. He heard the rest of the team in the shower. He sat at his desk going over the files on his players hoping that he would not have to send flowers to the family. He would have to push the team hard to win tomorrow, even if their star players were not there.

**~~

"LADIES AND GENTLEMEN. I HAVE NEVER SEEN ANYTHING LIKE THIS! THE MOCHIZUKI TWINS ARE HERE AND THEY ARE LEADING THIS TEAM TO TAKE THE TROPHY!"

The announcer yelled as Kenji scored yet again. The two boys had looked to the stands where their parents usually sat shocked that they were there. Their mother, pale and wan, waved her flag for her precious boys. Kouji ran down the field beside Kenji kicking the ball between the two of them.

"LADIES AND GENTLEMEN, THE FORWARDS ARE HEADING DOWN FIELD. WHICH ONE IS KENJI, WHICH ONE IS KOUJI? DOES IT MATTER? THESE BOYS ARE ON FIRE! WITH

THE OPPOSING TEAM'S STAR FOWARD OUT WITH TWO YELLOW CARDS THIS GAME IS FUJI HIGH'S"

Kouji kicked the ball, The goalie jumped shocked that the ball did not come his way instead it veered right as if it would miss the goal. Kenji dove in from the left kicking the ball past the goalie scoring the winning points with a few bruises on his knees.

The crowd erupts with cheers, banners flying as the home team took the win. Confetti began to rain down as music blared from the speakers drowning out the voice of the announcer.

"FUJU HIGHSCHOOL, HOME OF THE BENGAL TIGERS, WINS!!!"

Coach Tanaka ran onto the field with the rest of his team celebrating the winning of the tournament. He cheered as the twins were held aloft on the shoulders of the other players. This victory had been hard fought, the team played rough, yet they had persevered. Their high school had taken the trophy 3 years in a row.

"Alright boys, that was a fantastic game, well played." Coach Tanaka laughed. He gazed as his friends, the Mochizuki's, offering a soft smile. Come hell or high water they really had made it to every game this season. "I am proud of you all." He ushered the entire team to the center of the stand to receive their medals. Pictures snapped of those youth filled energetic boys as they clamored to place their lips upon their hard earned trophy.

Coach Tanaka stood behind his team after the kiss photo in order to take an official photo of the entire team with their trophy. Next he waved the Mochizuki parents over into the photo. He had known Mr Mochizuki since they had been in high school earning trophies themselves. The

Coach stood them behind their boys while the team surrounded them. With red rimmed eyes, their smiles were no less proud as they each held an arm around their boys.

**~~

Was this real? Kenji moved on instinct alone for his brain refused to accept what was happening. The world was still there. Kenji looked up at the sky in disbelief at the sun that dared shine on this day. This damnable day that he wished he himself had died. Kouji sat beside him in the police station staring at the officers as if they were speaking French. English and Korean and Japanese they knew. But these words, these heinous words he had no understanding of. The officer's mouth continued to move and yet nothing was making sense. Kenji held Kouji's arm while waiting for the officer to cease his speaking. "Kou?"

Kouji sat down beside Kenji. "They were on their way in a taxi to where Grandpa was in the hospital when a driver struck them. Neither made it to the hospital," Kouji broke then, sobs tearing their way through his body as he clung to his brother. Just yesterday they were on top of the world.

Their grandfather woke up. Their parents were going to see him and the boys would be along the following week after school ended. Then this, the terrible news of their grandfather going to bed for the night and not waking up. He had passed quietly in his sleep. While his parents were rushing to his side a wreck had stolen them from the world, from their boys. With a sigh, each boy stumbled into the van on their way to their home.

The house mocked them with it's silence. No one but the cat to greet them as they entered. Not an uncommon occurrence with their parents working as often as they did at his father's world shipping office. Yet this silence, this emptiness, this haunting echo confirmed that they were truly alone in the world. "Don't worry Kenji," Kouji firmed his spine as he held his brother close. "I'll take care of you." The way he said it, Kenji could almost believe it.

"We are only sixteen," Kenji did not remember sitting on the floor. He just looked up at his brother where he stood in their door that was still ajar. With the sun shining behind him he resembled a hero from a legendary tale in one of their mother's books. He often painted the fantastic scenes that she read to him. "How are we going to take care of the house? Shiro?" The cat rubbed her full form against Kenji where he sat on the floor.

The creature had been found as a tiny kitten out in the garden. Kouji went out looking for the mother and the rest of the kittens at his brothers insistence. He had told him that he never found them, in truth they were buried under the rose bushes. He did not have the heart to tell him that the poor little beasts did not make it.

"I called dad's brother, Uncle Monzo." Kouji explained. He sat beside Kenji on the floor as he could not get him to his feet. Kouji stretched out a hand to pet their kitty, sure the creature knew what fate his family had suffered at the canines of the neighbors mastiff. " He is on his way here." Kouji informed his brother. "Come on, let's go get all packed up. Lots of stuff to do before he gets here."

Kouji forged ahead. As long as he continued to move. As long as he had tasks to do, he could keep going. As soon as he stopped working, stopped moving then it would be real to him. They would be really gone. He would have to face the facts that not only had he lost his loving grandfather, but his adoring parents as well.

**~~

Kenji grasped his brother as they knelt by the photo of their parents. The candles and incense stung eyes already abused by grief. Only one other wake had they ever attended was that of their Grandmother Katherine. An American nurse stationed on the military base where she had met and fell in love with their grandfather. The two had wed producing one daughter, whose image smiled upon her sons from the photo as surely her spirit would smile upon them from the beyond. "Kou-Chan," Kenji looked down hiding the saline trail from any onlookers. "What are we going to do?"

Kouji's sigh was more of a sniffle. "I don't know Ken-Chan." Kouji trembled as the bell began to sound with the signal for the gathered mourners to rise and say their final farewells. "I think we are going to move in with Uncle Monzo," Kouji glanced back to where their father's brother sat with his arms folded over his chest. He seemed well-kept, though the boys had only ever seen him two other times in their entire life. Otherwise Monzo Mochizuki was a staunch politician attending many state affairs and traveling abroad.

Something about Monzo seemed off to Kouji. Cold. He wore a dark suit, with his hair cut close to his head. He was not an unattractive individual. He met the stare of his nephew with a slight nod of his head. Kouji shivered when those small, dark eyes found his own. "As long as we are together, we will be alright." The hall emptied of the well wishers and mourners leaving the two lanky boys and their uncle.

Mochizuki walked over to the young boys. "I know this is a difficult time in your life, yet we will make it through this, together." Mochizuki placed an arm around each slender shoulder. Though the boys seemed slight, their muscles were wiry and well defined after their many years of soccer. "I know being a politician must seem lofty to you boys, yet I will not allow your father's contracts to lapse. I will do my best to run the business until you are both old enough. Sayo and Keitaro will continue to grace us with their presence. Even if only it is their spirits watching over us."

    Kenji sobbed then leaning his head on his uncles' shoulder. The trio went out to the waiting luxury vehicle. The driver looked back at the two boys, a sad smile on his face. His crisp black and gray uniform gleamed in the light of the sun.

    "What will happen to our home Uncle Monzo?" Kouji asked the stern visage of their uncle. He had seen to their personal things being moved out of their home a frown on his face as the cat in it's carrier had been placed in his limousine.

"I know you grew up there," Mochizuki sighed. "I don't live in Kyoto, I live in Osaka. It would be best if we sold the home and you came with me. I have to get back to my duties, yet I can not in good conscious leave you boys here on your own. Don't worry there is a maid in my home so that when I am away, you will be looked after."

"Thank you, uncle." Kouji said with a sigh. Ever since their parents death, Kenji had said little, spending most of his time in his studio painting. The portraits and scenes dark, gloomy reflections of his broken heart. "Come on Ken-Chan," Kouji patted his brother's arms as it seemed their uncle stared at him.

"He seems slighter than you," Mochizuki placed a hand under his nephews chin lifting his face, he saw that the boys had their mother's eyes. The light reflected a pale green to Mochizuki as he looked at him. "You are the younger, right?" Kenji nodded feeling the stare of the older man down to the marrow of his bones. The hand trailed down his chin to his shoulder then his arm. "Don't worry, everything is going to be just fine. Let us get out of here, that cat has to be ready to be out of that cage by now. We will be just fine." Mochizuki promised. He licked his lips looking out of the window as he shifted upon the seat back to his own area. "Yes, boys, everything is going to be just fine."

Chapter 2

Mochizuki sat across from his nephews in the car watching as they silently gazed out of the window. Both young men leaned in close to each other a picture of youth so beautiful he sat down his reports and case files in order to watch them. Sometimes, when he received the holiday greetings and updates from his brother, he wished he had married, started his own family. Seeing these boys now, he wondered if he were being given another chance. Kenji leaned his head on Kouji's shoulder falling into a doze. Mochizuki noted the tears seeping from under his closed lids.

Kouji felt his brother sigh as sleep claimed him. It was more a sniffle than a sigh. He leaned down placing a kiss on his brother's head. He looked up meeting his uncle's gaze. "I am going to take care of your parents assets until you are old enough to assume responsibility."

"Thank you Uncle," Kouji nodded. Mochizuki noted the gentle manner with which he shifted his brother to a more comfortable position. "He can sleep in the most odd positions, then he is sore and cranky when he wakes." Mochizuki shifted upon the seat as he saw the two boys so close together. A plaintive mewling garnered their attention causing Kouji to place a finger in through an opening soothing their pet.

"I'm not home a lot," Mochizuki said with a soft smile as he gazed at the boys together. Their softness caused a thought to prick his senses.

"We won't be a bother," Kouji promised looking at his brother. "He is a studious kid, he will study and do his painting. I have my computer and we will pretty much try our best not to disrupt your life too much. I'll look after him."

"Well, who will look after you?" Mochizuki offered a sly smile. He tapped the drivers window. "Head to the Garden," The driver turned to face his employer. After a long look, he gazed at the boys, shook his head then looked away. His eyes glistening as he recalled his own time as a Flower in the Osaka Garden. "I just think it would be best if you lived in a place where you can be around some young people closer to your own age."

Kouji sighed. He felt his heart sinking as he gazed at his uncle; their last semblance of family in the entire world that they knew of. "You don't want us to live with you?"

"It's not that," Mochizuki assured the boys, he shut the screen of the door between them and his driver. "I just want what's best for everyone and I am more at the Garden than I am at home. When I am in town, I am there otherwise I am out and working. When I am home, I want to be alone. Don't worry you will not be a fruit, I know that you are not used to working so I will not have you as a fruit, you are too young to be a flower just yet," Mochizuki reached over to pat Kouji's knee. Comfort? Kouji fought the urge to move away from his uncle.

"What school will we attend?" Kouji asked after a moment.

"Tutors are sent to the Garden three times a week. Very exclusive tutors, only the best." Mochizuki explained. "I know that it will be a bit of a change, yet you will adapt to life in the garden, it is a very nice mansion. One could almost call it a castle. Fully appointed with anything that you could ever need. You will see. It will be much better than being alone in my boring old home."

Kouji nodded looking away from his uncle to gaze out of the window again. Many streets, with lovely houses passed by. Few pedestrians in this part of town at this time of day. Kouji glanced down at Kenji with a soft sigh. It seemed they would not have a home again after all.

**~~

Kenji awakened as the limousine pulled to a stop. "Are we home?" He asked with a yawn. Kouji dragged his sleeve over his brother's mouth, then wiped his arm on his pant leg. "Uncle," Kenji gaze at the grand edifice growing from the trees. "Is this your house?" Kenji gazed at the Mansion looming before them surrounded by trees. The traditional style abode showcased a myriad of trees surrounding the area leading up to the main doors.

The doors opened by a young man in dark blue uniform pants His gray jacket hung about his frame in lean lines while he rested a hand on his lower back in a bow. He looked up at Mochizuki. "Good evening sir and welcome to the Osaka Garden. Please enjoy your stay."

The young man bowed low he kept

his eyes averted from the Patron as he entered. He had worked in secret for many months when he was a fruit developing the muscles needed to become an animal as opposed to the delicate flowers. This phase of transitioning was the deciding factor as he was now old enough to enter into formal training.

"Tomoe," Mochizuki patted the young man on the head. "You have grown well since the last time that I was here. Quite lovely in fact. A bit tall though," Tomoe nodded his thanks. His face reddened as he hoped that he would not be found too attractive by the patron if he saw the evidence of his developing muscles "These young men are my nephews." Tomoe gasped as he gazed upon the boys. "They are not fruits and yet I will have them in the Iris suite with Keitaro. My home is no fit place for them. I trust you will make them welcome."

"Yes sir, of course." Tomoe turned to bow to Kenji and Kouji. "Are they flowers then?" He asked turning to lead the way down the fragrant hall.

"They are only fifteen years old," Mochizuki answered with a sly smile. Kouji hung back from the small group to look about the place that they would be staying. There was a level of opulence that was superseded by their own wealthy parents home.

"Sixteen," Kenji supplied their true age, "our birthday is in a few weeks actually." Kenji smiled at his uncle. "Why will we not stay with you?"

"This is more of a home than my place," Mochizuki explained to Kenji. "I just want to give you boys some place to be where you will not be so isolated and lonesome. There are plenty of young men and women here, why Tomoe is your age."

Kouji wondered why the young man flinched away from Mochizuki's touch. "You will be seventeen soon correct?" Mochizuki asked with a smile at Tomoe. The shining black hair bobbed when Tomoe nodded his head. Dark eyes refused to meet those of Mochizuki as he licked his lips in a nervous gesture the longer the patron stared at him.

"Is this an orphanage?" Kouji asked after they reached a room with emblem of an Iris carved into the wood. Tomoe opened it, bowing them inside. They found a honey haired young man inside poring over reams of sheet music. He glanced up. Large dark eyes widened as he saw Mochizuki standing in his door way. Yards of shining yellow and blue clothe shifted as he got to his feet. "Uncle?"

"Of course not," Mochizuki assured his nephew, "The Garden is ran by us patrons, you will not want for anything here. My house would be lonesome for you." Kouji nodded, he walked inside to see what the young man was working on. He could see that he was older than they were. "Keitaro, these are my nephews. Kenji and Kouji they are to live here, yet they are not fruits. Treat them kindly please."

"Yes, of course, sir." Keitaro paled as Mochizuki walked over to him. "I am already scheduled tonight sir. Katsu- Sama will be by in less than an hour to visit me." Keitaro was quick to say. Kouji wondered why the lovely young man would not meet his eyes. Pale cheeks bloomed with rosy color as trembling hands were hidden beneath his over long sleeves.

"Of course you have your regrets?" Mochizuki trailed a hand over the smooth cheek. " You will want to make it up to me surely?" Mochizuki smiled then squeezed the hip. "I will be by to see you this weekend." Keitaro sighed as his hair was stroked by Mochizuki.

"Yes, of course, sir. I will look forward to entertaining you." Keitaro tried to keep his voice from shaking as the rest of his body was.

"Better yet," Mochizuki looked at Kenji and Kouji. "Be prepared to go out when I do summon you. I will take you away for the evening." Sighing deeply as the boys were shown to the other room in the suite. "There is one bed in there now, however we can get two full sizes put in there for you. Surely you will not mind sleeping together." Kenji sat his bag down with a nod. "Your painting material and other belongings will be delivered soon. I must leave now and get back to work." Kouji nodded to his uncle as they went into their new room. "Your pet will be installed as well."

Dark wood paneling greeted them as sage green with yellow trim was painted along the walls. Several stands with vases full of irises reposed along with purple and yellow candles carved in the shape of the flower surrounded them burning with a soft glow ad cloying scent. The large, western style bed braced against a wall drew their attention with its purple and yellow gauze hanging from the four posts. Many pillows covered in satin were aligned to a point in the center almost shaped like a flowering bush.

"It's a nice room," Kenji sat on the bed. He looked around the various shades of green, white and yellow décor with hints of purple in the traditional room seemed to clash with the large western style bed. "That's a huge bed," Kenji walked around it running his hands along the dark wooden posts. "Even if they never get the two beds in here this one is big enough for four people." He flopped back on it with a sigh.

Kouji sat down Shiro's cage beside his brother. "We have to find a place to set her up with litter and food. Do you think Keitaro will mind our kitty? We can make this a home."

Kouji turned to look at his little brother. He was only younger by around fifteen minutes yet he would always be a baby to Kouji. "Leave it to you to find a positive." Kouji sat next to Kenji on the bed. "I'm going to look around a bit, you go ahead and get some more rest. I know you are still tired." Kenji nodded, kicking his slippers off he fluffed a pillow then leaned back. Shiro walked over to his head laying on the pillow beside him. Kouji stayed at Kenji's side patting his hair until his brother was sound asleep. Kouji wiped the tears that escaped from Kenji's eyes even in slumber.

Kouji left the room after covering Kenji to find Keitaro sitting in a chair staring out of the window. Kouji heard the sniffle on his way to the door of the main room. "Are you alright?" He asked walking over to where Keitaro was blowing his nose.

"Oh, gosh, yes," Keitaro wiped his face. Kouji sat beside him offering him another tissue. "I have to stop this. I have a patron visiting tonight, and Katsu-San will be most displeased if my eyes and nose are red."

"What do you mean, a patron?" Kouji asked. He started at the chime on the door. He watched as the young woman in the same uniform as the young man who opened the door hurried in pushing a cart.

"Thank you Kira," Keitaro smiled at her. She nodded, folds of deep brown hair falling over her shoulder. "She is fairly new here. Yoshinori found her working at her aunt's tea shop as pretty much unpaid labor.

She is sixteen, in another year they will begin her training."

"Training?" Kouji accepted the cup of tea from the beautiful young man. Keitaro smiled, his lush full lips curling upward to reveal dimples. "This is not an orphanage is it?" Kouji asked after a few contemplative sips. "It's a brothel."

"Surely you are too young to know of such things," Keitaro said biting into a deep, dark cherry. He made sure to stain his lips with the juice.

"I saw the way he looked at you," Kouji said with sigh. "When my uncle comes for you this weekend, he will have his way with you." Kouji sat the tea cup on the table marveling that Keitaro was so graceful.

"The Garden is not exactly a brothel," Keitaro explained. "We are kept here by the patrons. Our needs and wants are seen too, we are trained to pleasure them in many ways. When we are too old we are given a choice to stay or to leave."

"He said that we are not fruits," Kouji recalled his uncle's instructions. "What are fruits?"

"Kira, is a fruit now," Keitaro said after a moment. He ate some more cherries staining his lips deeply red. It was the behest of his visiting patron who preferred lips naturally red. "When she is seventeen she will begin her training to become a flower. If she develops muscles, she will be trained as an animal, that is highly unlikely, there has only ever been one female animal since I have been here. I am a flower. An Iris to be exact, the scent in this room and on this body is Iris. I specialize in decadence. Most of my accouterments are flavored. If you wanted a comparison in extravagance and decadent training, you could look to the Orchid suite, they are pale beauties in there. Goji has a new Bud to train. His name is Seitaro."

"Will we be..." Kouji could not finish his question. There was a light rapping at the door. Kouji inclined his head to the young man as he went back into their room. Crawling into bed with his brother, Kouji succumbed to his own grief.

Chapter 3

Kenji walked out into the bright sunshine with a gentle smile on his face. He saw Keitaro sitting at a table eating a simple breakfast of steamed rice, miso soup and grilled fish. A bowl of fruit sat next to his cup of green tea. "Oh... Good morning," Keitaro smiled when he noted his new suite mate walking with bare feet out into the garden. "Are you hungry?"

"Yes, I'm starved," Kenji bounced over to the table to sit with Keitaro. While they were there he hoped to make friends. He had heard awful stories of some teens sent to boarding schools that did not get along with their room mates that led to horrid living situations. It would be best if they could all get along.

Keitaro seemed so beautiful in the gleam of the sun surrounded by sweet smelling flora and verdant fauna. Small critters scurried about fat even in spring as the fruits left out food for them year round. Shiro sat at the glass door looking out. Her eyes darted over the scurrying critters.

"You must be Kenji," Keitaro said noting none of the sadness that Kouji had displayed as the two had passed each other on the way to the bathing room last night. Keitaro had just been left by Yoshinori and was in need of a bath. Kouji, with a sad smile had not met his eyes. The light in

Kenji's eyes shone with an innocence that Keitaro new would be ruined ere too much longer had passed.

"Wow, you can tell us apart?" Kenji smiled drawing Keitaro's eyes to the soft lift of his pink lips. Kenji was just bringing his chopsticks to his mouth when Kouji stumbled out of the room onto the veranda. He looked around the garden in the early stages of spring blooming. "There is plenty." Kenji assured his brother as he sat at the table close to them.

"Don't wander around without me," Kouji said with a hand on Kenji's arm. Kouji glanced over at Keitaro. He saw the mouth shaped bruise on his slender neck. Looking away Kouji muttered a greeting. He clasped his hands together in the traditional thanks for food.

Kenji frowned over at his brother as he began to partake of the well made breakfast. "What do you mean, don't wander?" Kenji chuckled after swallowing. "I am sure this place is safe. Uncle would not leave us here other wise." Kenji paused as he poured a cup of tea for Kouji. "I was looking around, I do not see any space where we could kick a ball around some of the paths here are a little wider, but we will have to careful not to damage any plants. All sorts of other hobbies and even a treadmill, but no court. There is a gym but it has mostly exercise bikes and treadmills, not weights or anything."

"We can't do anything that will leave bruises," Keitaro explained. Knowing that the treadmill was simply if some of the flowers put on too much weight. There was a Gym with weights and staffs for hand to hand combat practice, yet it was locked at all times and only the animals had the key. They were responsible for the maintaining of the equipment and the cleaning of the room as even the fruits could not enter for fear that one would work out and ruin their chances of becoming one of the soft, slender flowers.

"Oh, then... how...?" Kenji shushed as Kouji placed a piece of sliced apple in his mouth before he could ask about Keitaro's neck.

Kouji sighed. "On nice days you can set your easel up right out here." Kenji looked around the garden appreciating the blooms as they awakened in the onslaught of Spring. The air had the sweet smell of the many flowers in bloom.

"Do you believe uncle really thought that we would be lonely in his home?" Kenji asked after a few moments of eating in silence. "I'm never lonely when I have my brother with me." Kenji said to Keitaro when Kouji still said nothing. Keitaro smiled keeping his face calm as he thought of his impending time with Mochizuki. As a patron he paid he dues. As a citizen he obeyed all laws. As a business man, and politician, he performed all duties with a level of excellent competence. In the bedroom, he was akin to a barbarian.

    Keitaro recalled his first time with Mochizuki, a mere 2 days after his blossoming, the time when the Buds completed their training. He was still shy of his own pleasure, yet eager to experience more of what he had experienced with Ichi. While he had not finished as he so often had with Ryu, his trainer, he knew that he could experience pleasure with a man.

    Mochizuki had come into his room with a sly grin. There was no passion, there were not soft, sweet kisses to prepare and arouse the flower. Shoving Keitaro to the bed he had not even removed the elegant ensemble. Ryu heard the screams as Mochizuki pushed the robe up to Keitaro's hips and unzipped his own pants.

Thinking of the memories, Keitaro sat his chopsticks on the table. With a slight bow he stood to excuse himself. "You know you should eat more," Kenji and Kouji both looked up at the unfamiliar voice. Both boys stood to bow to the older young man. "Sit, and eat Kei-Chan," Skeins of shining obsidian colored hair fell over slim shoulders. The hair highlighted the pale face with soft features and deep set dark eyes shaped like almonds. The young man in the deep blue kimono admonished Keitaro with a gentle hand on his shoulder. The newcomer folded his hands into his sleeves before he turned to Kenji and Kouji. "I am Goji, I live in the Orchid suite, this is Seitaro," He introduced the boys to the young man in the white satin robe next to him.

Kenji could feel his mouth fall open as he saw the pale beauty standing next to Goji. The taller young man was handsome, yet this young Seitaro seemed almost inhuman with his snow white skin, raven's black hair and sweet, dark eyes. He had himself effectively hidden behind Goji until he was introduced. "New buds?" He asked indicating the twins where they sat ogling the young man that was only slightly older than they were

"NO!" Kouji lurched to his feet. He yanked Kenji up with him. "No... We are not buds." Kouji shook his head. He took the plate that they were eating then stomped with his brother back inside to their room. Kenji looked behind him a sad smile on his face as he gazed at Keitaro. Keitaro paused he watched the door shut. Tears fell from the green eyes so at odds with the features on the young man's face.

"That one knows more than he lets on," Goji said sitting in their vacated seat after holding a chair out for Seitaro. "I do like the Western style table out here."

"If they are not Buds," Seitaro spoke for the first time moving his sleeves back so that he could expose his hands and hold his chopsticks. "Who are they?" Keitaro smiled at the softness of his voice, he was sure the patrons would be enamored with him.

Keitaro sighed, "They are Mochizuki's nephews."

Goji choked on his tea. "Are you serious?" He looked inside even though he could not see the young men cloistered in the halls of the elaborate home. "I know his brother and sister in law died. I thought he would take them to his own home, not here. Gosh, why here?" Goji felt tears threaten as the smallest fruit ran forward with a cup of tea for him. "Thank you Dani," Goji addressed the child. Seitaro smiled. He was always amazed at Goji's level of poise and attention to detail. Seitaro smiled at the child as he blushed while scampering away.

"He did not want them to be lonely," Keitaro said. "Makes my flesh crawl thinking of them here." Keitaro shuddered staring with distaste at his food.

"Surely Mochizuki will not..." Seitaro ceased his question as he had heard of the brutality of their patron. "They are his brother's children."

"It matters not to him" Keitaro said eating when Goji fed him some of the eggs.

"Do you want to be back on the special diet to help you gain weight if you lose again?" Goji asked recalling the patron's displeasure as Keitaro had ceased eating for a while. Keitaro shook his head taking his chopsticks in hand he finished his breakfast forcing bits of food past the tightness in his throat.

**~~

Kenji sat watching as the child pushed the cart away carrying their lunch trays. For three days now Kouji had insisted that they take all of their meals in their room. He sat his paint brush down after staring at his canvas for over half an hour. "What's wrong?" Kouji asked sitting his book aside.

Kenji pulled his apron off before he sat on a pillow in front of his easel. "What's wrong?!" He faced his twin. So much more than his brother. Kouji felt like the missing piece of his own heart. "I'm going nuts in this room. We are not prisoners. Uncle did not say that we could not leave this room."

"That may be true," Kouji said keeping his voice calm as he heard their door open. "Yet I would feel better the less we have to do with this place until we leave."

"Leave?" Kenji and Kouji both turned to see their Uncle standing in their doorway. His suit was no less expensive than the last time they saw him. The brushed silk a watery pewter color. The glint of his jewelry glimmered at his wrists as the foreign watched ticked out the time. "You just got here, and too young to be on your own. The lawyer already brought over the required forms. You are legally in my custody until you are old enough to take over your father's business. In his will you will reach your majority at the age of 23. I think you can not hide in this room until then. You will either sicken or go mad." Mochizuki observed them both as they stood to their feet. He had wondered why neither had made a fuss about having a separate bed brought into the room. There was certainly enough space for one to be placed in here.

    Kouji saw Keitaro standing pale and trembling next to Mochizuki. Mochizuki turned to see the yellow satin of his kimono fluttering at the full body tremble. "I... I look forward to sp...spending the evening out with you." Keitaro swallowed bile at the hand that gripped his elbow. He knew that he would have a bruise as Mochizuki felt his shaking. While the other flowers took pains to make sure that Mochizuki did not know that he was least favored, it was still obvious in the fear that Keitaro could not hide. Kouji glanced away as Mochizuki took Keitaro from their room, then the suite.

"He is going to hurt him," Kenji said with a sigh. The few times he had managed to speak with the Iris Flower it was to find him soft spoken and gentle. The two had spent time going through his sketch pad. One of Kenji's paintings of a peacock surrounded by flowers was hung over the mirror in Keitaro's bedroom. "The other patrons seem almost kind yet uncle is feared. He is not good to them. The flowers I mean."

"You know what this place is?" Kouji asked sitting on the floor next to his brother. He had done his best to keep the true nature of this place from his twin.

"I'm not stupid," Kenji said with a sigh. "Just because you are fifteen minutes older than I am... I may never have kissed a girl before but I know what a hickie is when I see one. Since we have been here, he has sported quite a few. Either from a patron or Goji."

"Shit," Kouji sighed pulling Kenji into his arms. "I won't let them hurt you. No matter what." Kouji promised quelling the tremors in his own heart as he thought of the five men that would rule their lives until they were fully grown.

"Our uncle is a patron here," Kenji said shaking his head. "Surely they won't..."

"It is uncle that I fear most of all,"

Kouji confessed having caught his uncle staring at Kenji on the few occasions that they had seen him. Over the past few months he had been in town on rare occasions and true to his word he did spend his time in town at the Garden as opposed to his own home. "Just promise you will not be alone with him." Kenji gasped looking up at his big brother. With no words, he nodded his head.

**~~

Nightmares, whether waking or sleeping Kouji would wake with his clothes wet and tangled in blankets. Over and over again he saw the mangled car with his parents inside. Though they had been in Korea at the time and he had not actually seen them, he could well imagine a crash that destroyed them enough that they had not survived the trip to the hospital.

Kouji walked from the bed to their

shared bathroom. The door was slightly open. Kouji walked over. He could hear voices. Soft voices, the mingling of Orchid and Iris scents swamped his senses.

Kouji stood in the beam of light to see Keitaro sobbing in the sunken tub while Goji knelt at the side. The Orchid soaked a sponge into the water careful to keep the sleeves of his own robe out of the water. The soft sponge was dragged over the pale skin mottled with bruises.

Kouji stared in horror at the marks along the smooth skin. Was he bitten in some places? He knew that he should walk away, he should leave. He should afford them privacy, this was a bath. "Did uncle do this to you?" He asked softly walking forward his feet warmed by the heated tiles of the bathroom floor. The heated tiles had seemed beyond decadent to Kouji when they had made the discovery.

Keitaro continued his sobbing unable to answer as Goji cleaned a few more marks. "He did." Kouji sank to his knees beside Goji. With gentle hands he lifted Keitaro's arm to see the bruises and marks. Blood colored the water seeping from inside of him.

"Not every patron here is so rough," Goji said with a sigh. "For the most part we live a life of indulgence and pleasure. A small price to pay when you think of the alternative." Kouji gasped as he stared at the Orchid. "We all have our burdens. If we must suffer him on the rare occasions..."

"I'd rather be dead," Keitaro exploded. In a rush of water he stood from the tub. "I wish they had left me where they found me, God, why didn't I just die with the rest of them?" Keitaro broke into sobs. He limped from the pool treating Kouji to the sight of his small bottom. Deep purple hand prints and scratches scoured the terrain. Pink tinted water dripped from inside of him. Goji stood then to wrap his distraught friend in his arms and a towel. Keitaro stood in shock at the evidence of his uncle's brutality. How could he do that? What had he done? Is that really how he got off? To hurt someone?

Goji returned to the bathroom after tucking Keitaro into his bed. He sighed, then dragged a towel over the tile drying the drops of water. "His parents were partners of the Genzo family. Their stock and trade went under. In a last minute bid to save their business his parents and older brother boarded a plane to Nagasaki. Keitaro was home sick with his grandmother. He never saw them alive again. The plane went down.

Shortly after losing the rest of his family, Keitaro's grandmother died. He was seventeen when moved into the Garden and was trained immediately." Goji finished cleaning the water up not wanting to awaken a fruit this late. " You should get some sleep. I will go dry his hair. He has lost so much weight, the slightest chill will more than likely cause pneumonia."

Kouji nodded. He was quick as he washed his face. Kouji left the bathroom stopping in his tracks to see Goji standing in the open doorway to Keitaro's bedroom. His face ashen he turned to face Kouji. Kouji had seen that look before, that stark look of horror. "What's..." Tears cascaded from Goji's eyes in a panicked moved that Kouji never thought to see from the almost staid, mature young man. Goji sobbed as he rushed forward dragging Kouji back to his room.

"Stay in your room, oh God, stay in your room!" Kouji gasped as the door was slammed. "Don't come out! Oh Kei-Chan. What did you do?" Goji could be heard leaving their door. Kouji backed away from the door as he heard the commotion on the other side. Sirens, patrons, other flowers, they all trooped into and out of the suite.

Kenji awakened shocked when his brother blocked the door not allowing him to leave. "I don't know what is going on." Kouji explained. "I do not think we want to know. Goji said to stay in here and this is where we will stay until he comes for us."

"But... What..." Kenji choked on oxygen when Kouji dragged him back to the bed.

"I don't know," Kouji began to weep. "I have my suspicions but I hope that I am wrong." Kouji held Kenji close. "The police were here, I don't know yet if the coroner will be needed."

"What?" Kenji looked to the closed door. Trembling as he heard the troop of feet throughout the suite all night.

**~~

"Good morning," Kouji looked up at the stranger in their room. He stood in the traditional kimono of fine craftsmanship the white and red designs highlighted by his gray and yellow obi. Gold braided cord encircled the obi as he walked in on geta sandals he clasped his hands in a traditional bow of greeting of which Kenji and Kouji reciprocated. Kenji then sat at his desk with the homework that the tutor had left for them. "I am Ichi Genzo. My family is one of the founding patrons of this domicile."

"It is nice to meet you. I am Mochizuki Kouji," He shook the middle aged man's hand. He seemed very well kept, with a neat hair cut over trim brows and deep set eyes that seemed gentle in his middle aged face. "This is my little brother Kenji." Kenji paused in shaking his hand as he saw the somber expression on the older gentleman's face. "Is everything alright?"

Ichi sighed looking at the young men. They were beautiful in their own way. Two boys with the best of the genes that they were bred with. Creamy skin, with sandy brown hair and green eyes so incongruous with their distinct Asian features. Kouji moved his brother away from the staring, he stood tall keeping his brother behind him.

Ichi smiled, "we were going to place a second bed in there for you boys at your uncle's request, however," Genzo looked to the now locked door that was shut. "Once that room is cleaned one of you can be moved in there to give you more room."

"Where is Keitaro?" Kenji asked after a moment of staring at the closed door.

"He won't be staying here anymore," Genzo announced with a sigh. "He is in a hospital, last night he..." Genzo sighed shaking his head unable to speak of the incident. "As soon as the room is cleaned and re outfit, one of you can move in there." Ichi inclined his head to the young men with a sad smile he left the room.

"He tried to take his own life," Kouji said having heard the voices last night while Kenji had slept on. "He went into his room with a razor that is used to keep us smooth and he opened his wrists, Goji got to him in time and stopped the bleeding. They are committing him to a psych ward."

"What did uncle do to him?" Kenji's voice was a near whisper as he tried to force air into his lungs.

"Let's just hope that we never find out." Kouji sighed holding his brother close. "Gosh I hope we never find out."

Chapter 4

Goji paused before ringing the bell on the door. He had not seen either boy in over a week. The young fruit Dani was responsible for bringing their meals. He had told Goji of the paintings that Kenji worked on while Kouji spent hours with his computer. Goji pulled the bell smiling as Kouji opened the door. "Good afternoon," Goji reached out to shake Kouji's hand. Kouji paused feeling the soft appendage afraid that his rough hand would damage the soft skin.

"Hi," Kouji stepped back allowing him into his room. The shimmering cloth of the satin robe flowed about Goji akin like flower petals. The deep purple stood out in stark contrast to the white and pink cloth. While it seemed a lot of effort went into the outfit, it seemed as if it would fall from the slim form at the slightest provocation. "Nice to see you again. How is your friend?"

"It is nice to see you again." Goji smiled moving the ink black hair from his face. "Keitaro is healing, the bandages have come off. Katsu takes me to see him. He chopped off his hair before he got to his wrists. I'm sure that is why he is still alive, had he gotten to his wrists first, he would have bled out before anyone could help him." Goji walked over to the lounge area. "Keitaro had such beautiful hair."

Goji took a deep breath vowing not to weep again. He paused by the easel. Goji saw the Garden surrounding a bench. Some how the painting seemed so sad. "I was wondering if you boys had been given a full tour. I do not have any patrons visiting today and I am taking Seitaro to see the rest of the Garden. Would you like to join us?"

"Yes!" Kenji sat his brush down

rushing over to the door. He placed slippers on his feet shocked that their shoes had not been returned to them. The soft soled slippers were all that was currently available yet Dani had assured them that if requested they could be supplied. That was 2 weeks ago and still they had only slippers.

"So, I take it you would like to get out of this room?" Goji laughed. "Come along then. Seitaro should be finished with his bathing. He blossoms soon."

"Blossoms?" Kenji asked. Kouji shook his head when he thought of the implications of a bud blossoming in a garden. Kenji looked around the room seeing the well appointed hallway. He could smell the candles and incense that scented each room and the flowers that they were named for. Kenji saw a group of fruits hauling a cart into the room with a rose carving on the door.

"Kira is moving into the Rose suite today with Harumi." Goji explained. "I hear that the other room is all set up. Did you move in there?" Goji asked Kouji.

"His stuff did," Kenji explained with a chuckle. "For some reason he still sleeps in with me every night. I think he has bad dreams." Kenji recalled the first night of the second room being open. Kouji had set his stuff up then moved in. That first night, Kouji had walked into the room after Kenji got into bed. Crawling in with his brother he had held him all night, vowing to protect him from the monsters disguised as saviors.

**~~

Harumi walked along the path of the garden with Kira. She ducked as a ball whizzed past her head. "Oh my," Harumi giggled as she saw the rambunctious boys running through the flowers. Their blue shorts hung loose about their hips while their matching gray tank tops high lighted the soft tan of their peach toned skin. None of the flowers were allowed to wear sneakers yet the boys ran around in joy.

    Kouji had asked that their shoes be returned to them seeing as they were not flowers, the request was finally granted. Kira stared as the sun shone over them with a burst of laughter Kouji tackled his brother pushing him into the fountain. Kenji sat up spluttering and laughing shaking water from his hair.

    Mochizuki paused as he sat with Goji enjoying the garden breezes. He saw the light reflected off the droplets of water surrounding them. With a smile he continued to watch them. Goji gasped as Mochizuki got up to leave the garden without him. He breathed a sigh of relief flushing as Mochizuki turned back. He saw the smile of relief. How dare he? Mochizuki clenched his fists. His face reddened as he thought of the Genzo brothers calling on him in his office. They had approached suggesting that if he wanted to have a rough time that he visit another of their businesses, the Inu Koro Inn.

How did they think they could dictate to him how he used the flowers? They were there exclusively for their pleasure. He found the best ones, why that fruit, Dani, he had found him, and when he was trained it was Mochizuki that would demand to be his first. Mochizuki paused as he caught Kouji's gaze. He smiled at his nephew then glanced over at Kenji, the boys would grow well here, yes Mochizuki grinned. Very well.

**~~

Kenji dragged a towel through his hair as he left the bathing chamber, he paused seeing his uncle sitting in their lounge area looking through his sketch pad. "The paintings start here?" Mochizuki questioned. He moved over on the couch making sure there was room for Kenji to sit next to him. The dark blue couch had been adorned with yellow and white pillows matching the flowers in many vases around the room.

"Yes," Kenji draped the towel over his shoulder. He sat on the plush couch next to his uncle. Mochizuki closed his eyes sniffing. Mochizuki grinned as the iris scent clung to the young man's skin. Even though they were not flowers the only shampoo, shower gel and conditioner that was ever in this particular suite was scented like the blooms leaving the boys sweet smelling and alluring.

"You'll be seventeen soon," Mochizuki said running his hand through the damp hair. He knew that the boys had requested a barber to trim their hair, yet he had 'lost' the note. He jerked his hand back as the door to the other room slammed. Both Mochizuki and Kenji turned to see Kouji standing in his door with his arms over his chest.

"Did you finish the work that the tutor left?" Kouji said. "We have to keep up with our education. Can not take over dad's business without a functioning brain." Kouji joked shoving his brother from the couch. "And dry your hair, no need to catch a cold."

"I'm almost done," Kenji nodded, he grinned at his brother before he hurried to his room.

"And put some more clothes on," Kouji admonished seeing the thin robe clinging to his moist form after his bath. "You really will catch a cold."

"Yes, Nurse Kouji," Kenji sassed with a laugh. Kenji nodded his head smiling as he shut his door to find warmer clothes. His brother could be so fussy.

Kouji waited until the door shut before he went to sit next to his uncle. "Please," Kouji said after he sat the sketch pad down. "I know I have no right to ask, but please, leave him alone."

"What do you mean?" Mochizuki sat back with his arms folded. He had taken off his jacket not wanting to crease it. About once a month, he came by to visit them. He checked their progress reports from the tutors. Some times he would glance through the paintings, then even sit with them showing the profits from their father's business. Then he would leave, taking a different flower to his bed.

"Why him?" Kouji asked not bothering to indulge his uncle's question. "We look just alike, he is more sensitive, more vulnerable. If you want... I mean.

Leave him alone," Kouji swallowed the heave of his stomach. "Take... take me instead. If you... Whatever you did to Keitaro, if you do that to Kenji he won't be okay. The two of them are similar in mindset and temperament. Kenji is more competent and will more than likely succeed if he tries. I can't lose him too. If you want... Take me."

"I don't know what you mean?" Mochizuki looked over. "What you are suggesting..."

"I am not stupid uncle," Kouji said, he lowered his voice when he heard Kenji moving near the door. " I could please you. He has never even kissed anyone before. "

"But you have," Mochizuki grinned at his nephew. How could he explain it, it was Kenji's very innocence that called to him. He could show him so many things. Mochizuki looked back to the door again.

"How experienced are you? The Garden only ever accepts Virgins. I can not take you otherwise."

"I've kissed a girl, no more I swear. We are both pure. I will protect him. We are all that we have. Uncle Monzo. Don't do to him what you did to Keitaro. Whatever it is, I'll bear it, just don't take him. I couldn't bear to lose him too." Kouji closed his eyes as he got to his knees in front of Mochizuki. "I won't fight. I won't resist." Mochizuki stood to his feet. He passed a hand through Kouji's hair raising his face. He stared down into the deep, green eyes glistening with his un-shed grief. So dark and luminous, a perfect copy of his half American mother. Those lips. Mochizuki trailed his thumb over the full lower lip. He leaned in inhaling the sweet scent that clung to the flesh of the young man before him.

"You should have a bath," Mochizuki

looked into Kouji's eyes. "And get to bed early. Clean yourself well, there should be a white robe in the closet." Kouji nodded his head. He wiped the tears from his face with a trembling hand. If this is what it took to protect his brother, he would do it.

Kouji glanced at the closed door to his brother's room sighing. He would do whatever it took to keep him safe. He had watched after him for as long as he could remember, he saw no way that he could stop now.

Chapter 5

Kouji walked on silent, bare feet across the common room. He cracked the door open to Kenji's room glad the hinges were so well oiled. With a single minded determination he walked across the plush, gray carpet to the glass of water that Kenji kept by his bedside. He opened the capsule of sleep aid tipping the powdered contents inside stirring it briskly. He then dried his finger on his robe dark blue worn over the satin white one.

"What are you doing?" Kenji walked in after having cleaned his paint brushes.

"Making sure they brought you your water," Kouji said handing him the glass. "Drink it, the air is a little dry tonight." Kenji looked at his brother. Really looked at him. He saw the collar peeking under the usual bathrobe. His heart trembling at the sight of the white satin so like Seitaro's. Kenji nodded, not knowing what was going on, but not wanting to ask again what he had been doing. Kouji watched as the glass was drained. "Sleep well," Kouji tucked the blanket around Kenji.

"You are not sleeping in with me?" Kouji smiled as he was heading to the door. Kouji looked back at his little brother. Fifteen minutes may not be much time, yet in the grand scheme of their life, he was the older and he would always protect his little brother.

"Not tonight," Kouji patted his hair back. "You sleep well." Kenji nodded, feeling his eye lids droop as his brother left him alone in his room. For the first time in month's Kenji lay in his bed alone.

**~~

Kouji did not startle when his door was opened some time later. He sat his book down turning to face the door. Mochizuki gazed at his nephew feeling his face heat as he saw the bland acceptance of his fate. The pure white robe gleamed against his tan skin and honey colored hair so like his mother's. "Take off your robe." Mochizuki made his demand as he walked forward. "Repeat after me." The well made suit jacket was tossed over a chair. "I am Iris Kouji of the Osaka Garden," The tie was tossed aside.

"I am Iris Kouji, of the Osaka Garden." Kouji stood to his feet allowing the robe to fall to the floor baring his nubile body.

Kouji stood still hoping that the trembling was due to his lack of covering. "I will do all that I can to pleasure the patrons who graciously care for me."

"I will do all that I can to pleasure the patrons who graciously care for me." Kouji saw the belt come undone and the shirt tossed aside. He fought the urge to cover himself as his uncles eyes traveled over his body.

"My body is a thing of beauty, soft as a petal and just as fragrant," Mochizuki trailed his hand over Kouji's shoulder as he repeated the words. " I will never deny a patron my company, or my passion. I will not be touched by any but the patrons or my fellow flowers. This I vow until I leave."

Kouji closed his eyes as he recited the vows of the flowers of the Garden.. " I will never deny a patron my company , or my passion. I will not be touched by any but the patrons or my fellow flowers. This I vow until I leave." Kouji gasped as his mouth was crushed. Was this a kiss? When he had been with Ami, it was a soft sweet kiss as they had watched the fire works. He recalled the wonder of feeling her soft form in his arms.

Kouji pushed the tongue from his mouth with his own tongue. He shuddered as he had never felt so violated. Kouji choked on the tongue shoved past his teeth. Mochizuki pushed him back on the bed crawling over Kouji he grasped the firm behind squeezing.

Kouji gasped at the hands pawing his chest and his bottom. A severe pinch to the peak followed the mouth at his neck. Kouji grimaced at the wet invasion at his mouth again. He closed his eyes against the tears seeping out. Kouji tried not to cry out as he was bitten. He looked down at his chest to see the bruise left there and the brutal sucking on his nipple sure to leave more.

Mochizuki pushed Kouji's legs apart settling his weight between them. Kouji gasped, now? Like this? "No...Wait...Please" Kouji placed his hands on Mochizuki's shoulders when he left his mouth to suck and bite at his neck. Pressing forward he could not gain entrance. "Please stop."

Kouji raised his hand in fear that he would struck at the pure rage he saw glaring down at him. "Did you lie to me?" Mochizuki demanded with one hand he grasped the arm that Kouji had raised to protect himself from a blow. Mochizuki jerked the hand until he could look into

Kouji's eyes. "You said you would not resist."

"Please," Kouji bit his lip as he sat up on the bed after Mochizuki backed away. Mochizuki looked down to see what the young man was offering him. "I may be inexperienced, but I am not stupid. Please..." Kouji gulped, forcing saliva past the lump entrenched in his throat. " I am not resisting. I am asking for kindness."

Mochizuki took the vial of lubrication. He met those eyes. So like his mother. "You could have been mine, yet Sayo wanted nothing to do with me. I never understood why." Mochizuki said moments before he pushed Kouji back on the bed. "Turn over," Mochizuki demanded popping the cap open he kicked free of his pants. Kouji felt the oil applied. He may as well have not bothered with the negligent amount that was dripped onto Kouji. He gasped as hands on his hips pulled him back.

Mochizuki paused, should he do this? Did it matter? He felt himself engorged prepared to plunge in. His body dripping in anticipation. How could he resist such a soft form bent before him; ready to pleasure him? Mochizuki grinned as he gripped those slender hips. Using his thumbs to spread apart the pale cheeks. Winking there, beckoning him forth. With a salacious grin, Mochizuki thrust forth.

Kouji bit the pillow keeping his cries contained. He had ensured that Kenji would sleep, yet the sleeping pills could only do so much. Was he being ripped in two? The lubrication helped yet the pressure inside, the fullness... Kouji wept as each brutal thrust pushed him further to the edge of his endurance. Was he going faster? Kouji bit down hard on the pillow as he was taken with such force.

Stars seemed to dance before his eyes. "Why?" Kouji wept. He forced his head to turn until he could see Mochizuki where he was on his knees behind him on the bed. "I did not resist," Kouji gasped out. "Why so hard? It hurts. Softer please." He pleaded as his whimpering seemed to spur Mochizuki to go faster and harder.

"Quiet, I'm almost..." Mochizuki growled placing his hand on Kouji's neck shoving his face into his pillow. Held down he could see nothing but the sheets when he peeled his eyes open. Kouji cried out the more Mochizuki moved in him. Was he tearing? Is this why Keitaro was bleeding? Was he bleeding?

"It hurts, please," Kouji wept lifting his face up from the pillow. Kouji wriggled his hips hoping to free himself from the tight grasp, the burning pressure inside of his body.

"Just hold still and take it. I'm almost..." Kouji pushed an arm back hoping to dislodge his uncle. Mochizuki captured the arm keeping Kouji pinned as he reached his climax with a savage drive that left the young man splayed upon the bed.

Shoving free of the slight form Mochizuki stepped into his pants watching as, weeping, Kouji curled his knees to his chest. Without a backward glance he walked to the door. "Welcome to the Garden, Iris Kouji." Kouji covered his head with his blankets as tears escaped his eyes. Sobs wracked his battered body long into the night.

**~~

Kenji opened his eyes as the sun fell on his face. He yawned wide getting from the bed. It had been a while since he had slept that well. Kenji stretched looking around his room shocked that Kouji had indeed not joined him last night. He saw the Fruit, Dani, come into his room to clean up. "Ohayoo," Dani bowed low with a sweet smile. "You are alone this morning." Kenji nodded his head. "Will you have breakfast outside again?"

"Yes," Kenji nodded shoving into his slippers. "I'll go wake Kou-Chan," Kenji dashed across the common room. He tapped on the door instead of pulling the chime. Kouji groaned from beneath the covers. "Out of bed sleepy head." Kenji bounced on the bed.

"Oh... No... stop it," Kouji sat up wincing he placed a hand on his brother's arm holding him still. "What are you doing?"

"Get up," Kenji bounced off the bed. He noted the wince as the bed moved. Kenji stared in horror at his first look at his brother's face. " What happened to you?

Are you alright?"

"Yes," Kouji forced a smile noting as he did that his lips were swollen. He dragged his tongue across them feeling their tenderness. Kenji canted his head as he looked over his brother's bloodshot eyes. Dark circles with red veins covered his eyes. There were bruises on his neck. Kenji pulled the blanket down until he saw the bruises on his brothers chest and his waist. "I am starved. What's for breakfast?"

"What happened to you?" Kenji asked again after a moment. "You look like..." Kenji paused. He had seen that same glazed expression in Keitaro's eyes. The pain fogged hopeless stare was the same as the previous occupant of this room. "You are a flower now, aren't you?" Kenji could not hide the accusation in his voice as his brother winced refusing to meet his gaze.

"It was the only way," Kouji

continued to look away from his brother. With slow movements he pulled his robe over his body wincing as he realized just how sore his muscles were. "I am, and you are not."

Kouji could not ever recall seeing such a look of rage as crossed his little brother's visage. With flushed cheeks, eyes glistening he clenched his hands until the knuckles blanched. "You fool!" Kenji exploded as he stood from the bed feeling his heart accelerate he stared at his older brother. "Do you really think this will be enough?" Tears cascaded from his eyes, a lighter shade of green than his brother. " Now that one is in the other is soon to follow."

"I won't let them." Kouji stood from the bed. Kenji looked over his brother's body marked and bruised visible through the opening in the robe. "Why do you think I did this?!" Kouji demanded as he pulled a robe closed. Hiding his abused body from his twins eyes. "He said he would not come for you."

"He said... He! SAID!?!" Kenji raised his voice stalking forward he pulled the robe apart staring aghast at Kouji. His hips, his waist, his legs all were discolored and sore. "You think that means anything to him?" Kenji demanded. "For months now he has watched me. I saw it, I know what he wants. It's not just me that he wants, it's the thrill of the first time. May be he thought you were experienced; maybe he likes the gentle type and you seemed too tough for him." Kenji ran his fingers through his hair leaving the shorter strands on end. "You may have placated him for now. But it won't be enough."

"It will. Every time he comes I will..." Kouji ceased speaking at the very thought of Mochizuki touching him again.

Kenji shook his head. "Something is wrong with Monzo, Kou-Chan. He likes when it hurts. I saw it in what he did to Keitaro, you were sleeping but I heard him come back that night he was bleeding. Uncle told him not to carry it on, that he would be fine after a bath. He was not a virgin and he was bleeding. How rough do you think it was?"

"Believe me I know how rough it was," Kouji sat down his face paled as he refused to cry out in pain. He pressed his lips together. Kouji dragged a hand over his upper lip to dry it.

"We are his family and he would do this?" Kenji sat beside his brother careful not to jar the bed. "What makes you think that he will not take me too?"

"He promised," Kouji sobbed then giving in to the pain in his body and his heart. Kouji leaned over into Kenji holding tight as he released the sobs he had been trying so hard to hold in.

"Oh, Kou-Chan... In this," Kenji sighed. The hollow tone of his voice carried the loss of hope that they would make it out of the decadent prison unscathed. "You are more naive than I could ever be."

"You can't be a flower if you are not a Virgin." Kouji mused. "Go eat your breakfast. I am going to bathe, then I will join you." Kenji nodded.

"As I am neither a patron or a flower no one here will touch me." Kenji said getting to his feet. Kouji watched his brother leaving his room. Was it for nothing? Had he given himself for nothing? That much pain all for nothing? Kouji leaned over on the bed gripping the sheets in his hands as his battered body caved in to his tormented mind.

Chapter 6

Kouji sat back in the Garden watching as his brother cleaned his paint brushes. He had stood at the easel for over an hour and managed to prime the canvas. With a sigh he had given up on the endeavor. He saw his brother draped in the silken robes, his hair growing longer as he was no longer allowed to cut it. He seemed so soft now. Now that he could no longer kick the soccer ball around Kenji had no one to play with.

For weeks now, the other patrons had not visited. According to Harumi, most Patrons would wait to allow a flower to heal after they had been with Mochizuki especially if he was the one who was their first. How could they condone what he did to the gentle flowers? They allowed his brutality to carry on unchecked. Today, the reprieve would end.

"I'm going to the gym," Kenji announced. He picked up his shoes on his way out of the door. He paused as he saw Yoshinori standing in their common room. "I'll be awhile," He promised dashing down the hall. How had this happened? He ran down to the gym gasping as he sat on the floor near the treadmill. He could think back to this time last year. Was this when this path had started? When their grandfather had the first stroke, or before that? Was it when Grammy had died? Is that what started the downward spiral of their lives?

Grammy dying lead to Grampy's strokes which led to their parents going to Korea then led to the car accident and them being orphaned led to their being in Mochizuki's care and now this. That was the path of their life. How could they get themselves out of this mess that was The Garden.

Kenji stood to his feet. He walked for a few miles, before turning it to jog. He was in a full sprint when the door opened. He ignored Goji as the flower set up on the machine next to him. "How far will you run before it is far enough?"

Kenji slowed to a halt turning the machine off. He took a sip of water then faced Goji no longer shocked at how beautiful the Orchid was. Today his pants hung loose about his waist with an over large t shirt barely clinging to his frame. Feeling his own face heat at the peak of the chest visible under the thin material, Kenji looked away. "That's just it. I can not run far enough or fast enough to get out of this place."

"I am sure you realize it," Goji said after he stopped his own machine. He straitened the thick, messy braid that hung down his back. "The longer you are here, the more chances there are that one of the patrons will want you."

"I know that." Kenji sighed. "Kouji tries to keep it from me, yet I know. I see them looking." He walked over to a balance ball to sit. "The worst one who stares is Mochizuki, hard to believe our dad was his own brother."

Goji turned off his machine to walk over to where Kenji stretched. He straitened his shirt noting that Kenji put forth a mighty effort not to stare at him. "What will you do?" Goji asked.

"What can I do?" Kenji refused to weep. With a straitening of his spine, he walked to their suite for a bath. He saw the door to Kouji's room shut. With his hands over his ears he dashed into the bathing chamber. Sinking into the tub, Kenji allowed his turmoil to boil over with tears falling down his face he sat until his skin wrinkled.

After his bath, Kenji walked over to Kouji's door. He could not hear any thing. He reached for the door nob, halting as he heard the bed springs followed by a cry. Kenji leaped back from the door as if his hand had been burned. With his face inflamed, he dashed to his own room. Kenji sat on his bed with a book reading until his exhaustion left him curled up in bed clutching the book to his chest.

**~~

Kouji stood beside his bed. He could feel his heart pounding sure that Yoshinori, his first official patron, could see it outside of his robe. "You are trembling," Yoshinori said holding a hand gentle on the newest flower's face. Kouji could not seem to be still . Kouji allowed his face to be raised until he met Yoshinori's smile. "Be at ease, Iris Kouji. I will not hurt you."

Yoshinori sighed as he recalled Goji

explaining to him the condition of the Iris suite. So it was true. Kouji had been sorely used his first time. Kouji met the soft brown eyes. He took in the kind smile. This patron had hair cut close to his head his suit was well kept, expensive. The cloth rivaled some that his father used to own. Yoshinori could not be called handsome, yet his manners were elegant.

Kouji gasped as his face was brought forward. The lips that met his were gentle. The tongue did not force entry, instead it licked his lips until he sighed then slipped inside tasting the sweet nectar within.

Yoshinori backed away after licking his lips again. "After Goji told me what happened, I have kept the others at bay." Yoshinori smiled then. "Give me your tongue." Kouji opened his mouth. This time, when Yoshinori placed his tongue inside, Kouji responded. The tentative press of his tongue along Yoshinori's brought a sigh. "Yes little one, give it to me," Kouji gasped as Yoshinori sucked his tongue into his mouth before moving on to the lips. He felt the moment when Kouji gave in to his desire. The young man sighed leaning into him giving more of his mouth.

Kouji could not recall anything feeling so swell. He felt the soft, warm hands. Kouji paused at the hand inside of his robe. "Just relax." Yoshinori pressed his lips to Kouji's again. He moved down to his neck, tasting the little flower. Kouji moaned leaning into the embrace. He could feel his body heat the more the patron caressed him. That hand found the peak of his chest. Kouji yelped at the simple stroke.

Yoshinori moved down to taste the sweet peak. Laughing as Kouji collapsed on the bed. The surprise in his sweet green eyes drifted closed. Yoshinori smiled down at the new flower. He sat on the bed clutching his robe to his neck.

The bright yellow and green flowers over the sky blue satin made him feel as if he were in the forest. Yoshinori sat on the bed, glad that the patrons had installed western style mattresses. He placed an arm around Kouji taking his lips again he laid Kouji back upon the bed.

"Did he at least use something?" Yoshinori asked laying beside the supine form. He trailed a hand over the smooth chest. Kouji nodded as he surrendered to yet more kisses that stole his breath away. Kouji gasped again , moaning as that hot mouth made it to his chest. Instead of the bites and pinches, there was only pleasure and kisses. Kouji pressed his fingers to his lips. "No, let me hear that cute voice," Yoshinori grinned against the moist flesh as he dragged his tongue along smiling as another moan was brought forth.

Kouji did not know when his robe

was opened all the way. All he knew was that the tongue trailing down his body was lighting a fire within him. Kouji ran his fingers through the soft hair on top of Yoshinori's head as that wicked tongue delved into his belly button. "Oh... wait... what," Kouji gasped as Yoshinori began to fondle him. He was gentle as he aroused the flower for his first real foray into the sensual arts. Not even as he explored with his own hand had he felt anything as sublime as the mouth that tasted his most intimate regions.

Yoshinori pushed those slim legs further apart sucking in deeply. He heard the piteous mews of the young man. The more he sucked the larger he grew sinking into the mattress in full surrender. He knew it was coming, the end. How could a man bring him such pleasure. "Don't be afraid," Yoshinori coached. "Just relax and enjoy it." Kouji could only cry out as his body released.

Kouji opened his eyes to feel a soft hand caressing his face. "How wonderful," Kouji sighed returning the kiss. "Thank you." Kouji could feel the tears stinging his eyes.

"Just relax," Yoshinori intoned. He stripped from the rest of his clothing. Kouji knew what was coming. He braced himself on the bed. With his back pressed to the mattress he brought his hands up to the side of his head. With his legs bent at the knees and feet splayed he waited. "What are you doing?" Yoshinori asked. "No don't tense up. I just got you all relaxed." Yoshinori smiled down at Kouji. "I am not going to hurt you."

Kouji wanted to believe him. He knew of what was next. What Yoshinori would do to him. He tried to stem the trembling yet he could not seem to control his body. A soft smell found him.

Yoshinori spread the lubrication on his fingers. He reached down again stroking the young flesh to life again.

With a few deft movements, he had those slim hips rising and falling. Kouji began to moan again as Yoshinori brought him to the brink. Before he could give in to his pleasure he felt a finger pressing into him. "Now?"

"Relax, it won't hurt," Yoshinori promised. Kouji felt the finger, the pressure was there, yet different from the pressure of Mochizuki. He relaxed into the gentle insertion feeling his body open, accepting. "That's right, Kouji, just relax and let me show you."

Yoshinori inserted another finger. He spread them apart loosening the portal and spreading the lubrication inside. Yoshinori climbed on top of the lithe form. He pressed inside swallowing the cry as he pressed his lips to Kouji's.

Kouji could not recall ever feeling so good as he felt now with Yoshinori moving above him. The thick length inside of him was not tearing him apart, it stroked him in ways he could never have imagined. Kouji groaned pressing his knees against Yoshinori's sides wrapping his arms around his neck returning the kisses with all the innocent fervor he could muster.

Yoshinori smiled down as he took the sweet flower to the depths of ecstasy. Soon he would capitulate. Soon he would know physical completion. Yoshinori brought a hand between to ease the hardness straining and leaking on Kouji's stomach. He pressed their lips together taking Kouji all the way to the pinnacle of pleasure.

**~~

Several hours had passed when Kenji was awakened again. Kouji sat on the side of his bed. "Hi." Kenji yawned wide. He offered a sleepy smile to his brother. "What time is it?" Kenji wiped his eyes on the back of his hands. With a sniff he sat up reaching for the cup of water that Kouji handed him.

"A quarter to three," Kouji said peeling from his robe. "Listen to me." Kouji explained as he peered at his brother in the darkness. Kouji took the now empty glass placing it back on the night stand. "I figured it out." Kouji pushed Kenji back into the bed before crawling under the covers with him. "I know how we are leaving here. They will only accept a flower who is a virgin and if a flower is with someone else he or she will be expelled."

"What are you..." Kenji could not continue his question as his mouth was under his brothers. Kenji gasped feeling his brother's tongue slide between his lips. Kenji pushed Kouji back wiping his mouth with his hand. "What are you doing?"

"You don't even know how to kiss," Kouji laughed after a moment. He pressed into Kenji again. "Stop hiding your tongue from me. I'll show you."

"Stop it Kou!" Kenji pushed his brother off of him. "What are you doing? We can't this is wrong. You are my brother." Kenji struggled against the hold gasping as his hands were pressed to the mattress above his head.

"This entire place is wrong." Kouji fought to keep from yelling. "I am not letting them get you. This is the only way, now just relax. I won't hurt you."

"No!" Kenji lifted his legs tipping Kouji over. With his hands busy restraining Kenji, Kouji lost his balance. Kenji pushed Kouji away from him. He leaped from the bed leaving his slippers behind Kenji dashed off the bed to the large veranda doors and out into the garden.

Kouji called his name leaving from the veranda doors that opened amid the lush tapestry of the flowers still alive even though fall was coming to Osaka. Kenji ducked behind a tree falling to his knees. He peered as he heard Kouji running behind him.

"Kenji," Kouji called. "I'll be careful, but it's the only way." Kouji ran into the garden after Kenji. Kenji sat at the base of the tree sobbing. What madness was this? What had brought his brother to this conclusion? Was it their uncle? The rules? The patrons? Kenji bawled. He startled as he felt his brother's hand on his shoulder. "Don't fight me. It will hurt if you do."

"Kouji please," Kenji reasoned wiping his face on his sleeping robe. "Think about this rationally. We can't do this."

"I have thought about it," Kouji explained. "Come inside. It is chilly out here." Kenji got to his feet. "You will get sick." He walked beside his brother into their suite. "I have thought about this for many days. It does not have to be rough, and painful. It can be enjoyed. But I do not want you to live this life. I know Uncle will come for you. But only if you are a Virgin. The other flowers will not break the rules. Don't you see? We can both be expelled."

Kenji looked at Kouji. Deep into his eyes. He saw the trauma of the past seven months played out in his soul. First Grampy, then their parents, their home and all they knew lost to them. They were trapped in this false paradise of perfume and submission. Flowers caged in an opulent prison.

"Oh, Kou-Chan," Kenji wept. What had he sacrificed in his protection of his brother? How could Kenji ever repay the debt of Kouji allowing their uncle to hurt him so fully. Kenji sniffled as he held Kouji tight. "Alright," Kenji sobbed his answer. "I won't fight you." Kenji leaned back against his pillows. "What do I need to do?"

"Just relax," Kouji smiled at his brother. With a gentle hand, he wiped the tears from Kenji's face. "In the morning this will be a night mare and we will be free." Kenji nodded opening his mouth when Kouji pressed their lips together again. This time he did not gag. This time he did not hide his tongue, this time, he responded. Their tongues slid together in a sensual dual highlighted by the salt of their mutual tears.

"Whoa," Kenji sighed leaning back into the pillow.

"Right," Kouji smiled licking his own lips. "Feels good." Kenji felt his cheeks heat glad that there was only darkness to highlight his color. Kouji took Kenji's lips again laying beside him on the bed. Soft hands passed over Kenji's chest pushing the robe open. "First I will get you ready. It is easier to relax if you have experienced pleasure first." Kouji explained why he was touching him. "If I just take you, it ends your virginity, but hurts like hell."

Kenji nodded trying not to push the hand away as it caressed his nipple. "That feels weird." He whispered turning his face into another kiss.

"But not bad?" Kouji asked licking a finger tip he brought it back feeling the sensitive peak harden. Kenji shook his head moving his mouth under Kouji. Kouji then moved on leaving a soft kiss to his neck then his chest. Kenji gasped releasing a startled moan as Kouji licked his nipple. "Like that? Yoshinori taught me." Kouji stroked down the concave of the tummy while nibbling at the chest. Kenji jerked reaching down to hold the wrist of the hand encircling him. "Shhh... It's okay."

Kenji nodded his head forcing his fingers to relax even as his body stiffened. "I think..."

"Shhh," Kouji kissed him deeply again. "Just go with it." Kenji gasped as he sprung to life in his brother's stroking hand. "Open your legs, let me lay here," Kouji pulled the sleeping robe free of his brother's body as he lay on top him. Kenji gasped feeling the full hardness of the body above him. "Just relax. I am going to get you ready."

Kenji yelped at the wet fingers pressing inside of him. "Ow...Itai," Kenji gripped the wrist of Kouji's hand again.

"I have to start with my fingers," Kouji explained. "If I just go in it will get the job done, again, it will hurt like hell." Kouji reiterated. "Just go with it."

"Mmm...okay," Kenji released the wrist. He trembled as those fingers crept inside of him. "Ah..." He breathed deep. Kenji reached around wrapping his arms around Kouji's neck pulling his face down. "When you kiss me, it's seems okay." Kouji smiled down at Kenji. With a sigh he pressed their lips together kissing him fully. Kenji relaxed under him allowing his fingers to inch inside of him. The fingers expanded in girth. Kouji used his other hand to stroke Kenji keeping him aroused as he opened his body for possession.

"I'm ready, all lubed, Just relax, breath in," Kouji coached. He pushed in just the tip of his excited member. He felt the hands at his thighs pushing back, resisting. "I know, just relax, it will be okay, keep breathing." Kenji gasped biting down on his lip as another inch gained. Tears seeped past his eyes as he was fully claimed with one slow thrust. "How bad is it?" Kouji asked as he felt the trembles and sobs beneath him.

"Can we stop?" Kenji plead. "It's done now."

"I'm not leaving you like this," Kouji explained stroking the hardness between them. "It will stop hurting soon," Kouji promised as he shifted his hips. He pressed in again moving against his brother. "Raise your hips, move with me." He coached pressing their lips together. Kenji held on to his brother moving with him as the moon shone overhead. He began to pant as the pain lessened. There was still a deep pressure inside of him, yet it was not painful. Far from it.

Kenji's hips moved on their own. Shifting taking more in. He began to climb heights of passion he had never dreamed of with the use of his own hand. "That's right." Kouji coached feeling his own body capitulate to the tight enclosure. "Oh... Damn Ken-chan. This feels so good." Kouji gasped.

"Kou..." Kenji gasped closing his eyes against the stars that danced over his vision as his body exploded. He gripped Kouji's neck as he was stroked to completion.

"Damn... Damn.... Kenji!" Kouji grasped the hips holding them still as he peaked filling the tightness with his release. "Wow." Kouji collapsed beside Kenji on the bed. He leaned over him taking a tissue to clean the fruits of their lovemaking. Kouji pressed a soft kiss to Kenji's lips as he passed out in slumber. Kouji lay down then. Holding his brother through the night. Protecting him in the best way that he knew how.

Chapter 7

Morning found Kouji still in bed with Kenji. He pulled the blanket closer around him. "Mmm," Kenji moaned in his sleep. "I'm sore," He whispered nuzzling Kouji's neck.

"And a bit warm," Kouji wiped a hand over Kenji's brow. "We only have half of the problem solved." Kenji stood from the bed. He was pulling his robe on as the chime on the door sounded. "Say nothing of this for a bit, let me figure out how to present it so that we can both get out of here." The chime sounded again. Kouji hurried over to open it. "Shhh, he doesn't feel well."

"Shall I ask for a physician?" The fruit asked wheeling in his cart with their breakfast.

"No," Kouji smiled. "I'll tend to him. Request that I not have any patrons today owing to my brother not feeling well. I will keep him in bed and take care of him. You are Dani right?"

"Yes Iris Kouji," Dani nodded bowing his head until the short bob of ravens black hair covered his reddened cheeks.

"Please see if Goji can come by today?" Kouji asked looking to where Kenji pulled the cover up past his chin to cover his eyes. "Also, a bath please."

"Yes, Iris Kouji." Dani bowed from the room leaving his tray behind. Kouji pushed it to the bed.

Once Dani had left, Kouji propped a pillow up behind Kenji. "You did not tear last night, or bleed." Kouji handed him a cup of tea. "There is Gentian in this. I use it in the mornings to relax. It will help." Kenji nodded sipping. "Why won't you look at me?"

"It's wrong," Kenji sobbed. Kouji was quick to take the tea cup before it could be spilled in his brother's lap. "It's all so wrong. We shouldn't even be here."

"But we are," Kouji sipped from his brother's cup. "For whatever reason, we are here. What's really wrong with you?" Kouji asked as still his brother sobbed refusing to look at him.

"It... Well..." Kenji sniffled he gripped and released the comforter. "Last night," Kenji broke then throwing his arms around Kouji's neck. "It felt wonderful and I know that it was wrong...I... I came... It felt amazing and I know it should not have..." Kenji stopped speaking as his mouth was claimed. He responded to the kiss with a broken surrender of all that he once held dear.

**~~

Goji entered the Iris suite in a hurry. "Dani rushed in this morning, he said you needed me. Seitaro blossoms today. I have to get him ready." Goji walked across the room into Kenji's room. He pushed past Kouji. "What did you do?" He asked after seeing the flushed cheeks and bruises on his neck. Kenji avoided eye contact with Goji.

"What I had to," Kouji blushed looking away. He could not face his brother or fellow flower with the truth of what he had done. "Neither of us are fit to be flowers here."

"No," Goji sat down on the bed. He lowered his head to his hands. After a moment he patted the trembling hand of the young man still in the bed. "You should have asked for my help before. Now I can just barely repair the damage."

"What do you mean," Kenji asked

seeing the tears as they gathered in Goji's eyes. "Kenji will remain here as a flower, you will be condemned to the Inu Koro Inn, it is a vile place full of sadist who enjoy inflicting pain."

"Our uncle must be the best guest on the list," Kouji said his cheeks flushed with rage as he gripped the robe until his knuckles turned white. He recalled the feeling of the negligent amount of lubrication that was used for his first time compared to the care that was taken his second time. "All I did, I did for nothing. If they would banish me, fine, I'll take it. But let him go."

"You don't want that." Goji got to his feet. He looked at a clock on the wall. "Confess then, I need to hear you say it," Goji sighed.

Taking a deep breath Kouji looked over at Kenji then back to Goji. "I deflowered Kenji last night," Kouji admitted.

"I figured," Goji nodded with a sad smile. "Probably the gentlest claiming we would have seen in a long time." Goji stood to his feet. "All of the patrons will be in attendance tonight for the claiming of Seitaro, if I can get Yoshinori alone, he may be able to help you." Kenji nodded his head. "Eat your breakfast." Goji got to his feet he looked back at the boys from where he stood at the door. Shaking his head, he smiled at them then left them alone. Kenji and Kouji were both beautiful in their own way. He hoped to have a taste before he left this place.

**~~

Yoshinori folded his hands as he entered the suite. He recalled Kira approaching him with a slip of paper from Goji requesting his presence. The bottom of the paper had a small Orchid flower drawn on it with the request to destroy the missive. Goji walked past the fire pit in the garden dutifully tossing it in before he rapped on the glass door of the Orchid suite. Goji sat down his brush rushing to open the glass panel doors. "Thank you so much Yoshi-San," Goji bowed ushering him into the the opulent suite. "O-Sei, why don't you go practice the Vow, we want it perfect."

Seitaro nodded making sure the sash of his robe was aligned. "What is the matter? You are shaking." Yoshinori asked leading Goji to a corner in their common room as he figured the garden would not be a safe place to be discussing whatever needed a destroyed missive. "What have you done? Is Seitaro not a virgin?"

"It is not to do with O-Sei," Goji assured the patron. "He is most nervous, yet I have assured him that Katsu will be gentle with him. The problem lies with the Iris suite." Goji lowered his voice. "You know Mochizuki took Kouji, the experience was not something he would have his brother suffer through."

"Oh no," Yoshinori sighed recalling his night with the flower. He had taken his time to show him that physical closeness could be enjoyed.

"They are terrified now, I need not tell you what happened."

"No, I get it." Yoshinori got to his feet. "If Kouji is sent to the Inu Koro, even as he ages out his claim to the family businesses will be lost as it is public who is there, here there is privacy and a sort of honorable sanctity. There, the depravity is beyond reprehensible and I would not have either of them there. Do you know what Scat is? Or golden Showers?" Goji shook his head in terror at the disgust he could feel in waves pouring from Yoshinori. "And God willing you never will. I can help them. I will make it known that having one, I must have the other. I will be Kenji's official first."

"But..." Goji sighed.

"No, we have no way of proving it. I will go down as blossoming him. I will also buy their father's business. If they agree to stay here until they are of age, then I will sign it over to them when they leave. I will fight Mochizuki for custody. I am a lawyer, you know that."

Goji wiped his tears. "Thank you." He pressed a kiss to Yoshinori's lips.

"Of course, now go," Yoshinori got to his feet. "Make sure your bud is ready to blossom in style, while I go and save those two kids from themselves." Goji smiled over at Yoshinori before he headed back to Seitaro. "I will declare for Kenji, and be his official first. Surely Monzo anticipated this when he brought them here."

"I am sure this is exactly why he brought them here." Goji sniffled.

"Repair your face before the others get here. You are to be presenting your Bud tonight." Yoshinori got to his feet. "After he says his vows I will let them know that I was approached by Kenji to join as a flower and agreed to honor it. Kouji can serve as witness." Goji nodded his head with a smile.

**~

Dani took a moment to straiten his top before he rang the chime. Tonight he recalled being stared at by several of the patrons. He would be an animal before he would ever wish to be a flower. Something about allowing them to fornicate with him chilled his blood. Dani saw the boys both sitting in the lounge. They sat on opposite sides of the couch.

Kouji sat down his book while Kenji put aside his pencil and sketch pad. "Hello Iris Kouji and Bud Kenji," Kenji gasped at the title. "I bring you news of your blossoming, it will be tonight. Patron Yoshinori will be here soon to uh... Well. He will be here." Dani bowed.

"Wait... No," Kouji caught Dani's arm. "No, he has to leave here." Kouji looked at his brother. "He can't stay. We... so that he could leave, we... He has to leave." Dani puffed up as if to explain yet the door opened behind him.

"You should be quiet," Goji said after he looked down the hall. Looking at his elaborate kimono Kouji grew silent as the Orchid shooed Dani from the room. "You know these walls are well made yet shouting in the lounge will definitely carry." Goji ushered the twins to the couch where he sat between them.

"What have you done?" Kouji asked feeling his eyes brim. He sniffled as he recalled the moment he had tried to save his brother from the bully at their school and ended up with a black and suspended from school. He had taken it knowing full well that the bully would never pick on his brother again.

"I cleaned up your mess," Goji placed a finger on Kouji's lips when the young man would have said more. "As it is what you did put you guys in more harm than good. According to the will you both inherit, if one can't then neither will unless the other is dead. You are still very much alive, yet being confined to the Inu Koro you would be registered there in the AV industry you would never be able to run the business once you leave there. Not all of the acts committed there are gross, just recorded and sold to the market at a profit."

Kouji gasped as he realized that if he could not inherit while alive, Kenji would not be able to inherit until he was dead. "I would rather be dead than ruin his chances." Kouji sobbed at the hopeless situation he had created.

"Stop it Kou!" Kenji stood to his feet. His sweat pants seemed so out of place in this domicile of satin and lace. "Who made it so that you have to decide? What law says that you decide our future? You decided we would play soccer, I wanted basketball. You decided what color our rooms would be at home. Now this is home. Just because you were born first doesn't make you older."

"Yes," Kouji faced Kenji. "It does! I am fifteen minutes older than you are." Goji tried his best not to laugh as they continued their bickering.

"That is not the point." Kenji sighed

as he vowed to make this right for them. " I would rather stay here with you as a flower than have you in some brothel where a sicko smears shit on you." Kouji gasped staring at his brother. "Scatting... I looked it up." Kenji narrowed his eyes. "Also known as corophilia. Don't even get me started on Golden Showers, I'll give you three guesses. Or did you suddenly become a deviant and being pissed on gets you there? In all honestly this place is a dream compared to the alternative."

"Your brother is right," All three looked up as Yoshinori walked in the room. "You know these doors don't lock." Yoshinori walked over wearing his families uniform from their days as Imperialist during the Meiji era when the Garden was first established. The maroon and blue traditional ensemble suited him well.

"Any one could walk in and all Goji and I have done, all you have done will truly be for naught. I am suing your uncle for guardianship of you and buying your dad's business. It will be yours when you leave here depending on the manner of which you leave. If you serve your term, then you will be free, and the business yours. It was the best that I could do. If they find out you flaunted the rules and had sex with a non flower or patron, you will go to the Inu Koro and Kenji remains here as a flower. Never to inherit so he would be here forever, like Sakura Haru. Though in his case it is by choice."

"So that's just it then?" Kouji sank to the couch with his head in his hands. "We did the unthinkable and it was for nothing."

"At least we will be together," Kenji sat beside him. He leaned his head against his brother sobbing as well.

"Go bathe," Yoshinori inclined his head to Goji. "We have to go now. Teach him his vows, I will expect to hear them later." Yoshinori passed a hand over Kenji's hair until he could raise his chin. "You will enjoy it with me. I promise." Yoshinori winked as he walked out of the Iris suite. He would make sure that they all enjoyed themselves tonight.

Chapter 8

Kenji sat still as his brother brushed his hair. "Yoshinori will not hurt you. Your first official time will be pleasant. At least there is that. " Kouji promised. He smiled as he pressed his lips to Kenji shocked when he did not turn away.

"My first time was pleasant," Kenji reached for the lip gloss after he backed away from Kouji. "Thank you for that. At least I came."

"More than I can say of my first time," Kouji sighed sitting beside his brother. He recalled the brutality of his own blossoming.

Kenji shook his hair from his face. "Our time here will be just a night mare when it is all over."

"If it is just a dream," Kouji sat beside Kenji as they awaited their guest for the evening, "Then we may as well enjoy it." Kenji pulled Kouji's face close to his own for a soft kiss.

Yoshinori entered the Iris suite. He paused as he saw the boys close together. Their hair the same shade caught the dim light reflecting it back as if sunlight poured over honey. Identical faces turned towards him their eyes various shades of green limpid as they licked well kissed lips. "Come Bud Kenji, recite your vow to me."

Kenji stood to his feet brushing the

white robe he wore with his damp hands until it fell in soft folds to his feet. "I am Iris Kenji of the Osaka Garden," Kenji began to say the vow as Kouji has taught him. He glanced at his brother.

"I will do all that I can," Kouji prompted him with a nod of encouragement.

"I will do all that I can to pleasure the patrons who graciously care for me." Kenji said with a deep breath. "My body is a thing of beauty, soft as a petal and just as fragrant."

Kenji paused nibbling his lower lip. Kouji smiled at him holding his hand. Kenji looked over at his brother. " I will never deny a patron..."

Kenji nodded with a soft smile he continued. "I will never deny a patron my company or my passion. I will never be touched by any but the patrons or my fellow flowers. This I vow until I leave." Kenji finished his recitation with a deep breath. He trailed his tongue over his lips then glanced at Yoshinori. "Now what?" He asked after a moment.

The smile was gentle. "Now we make it official," Yoshinori took Kenji's hand pulling him to his room. Kouji stood back blinking tears from his eyes seeing his little brother lead away. "Come Iris Kouji, you will bear witness," Kouji gulped as he followed Yoshinori and Kenji into his room.

The warm, soft glow enveloped them in the scent of iris flowers and candle wax. Several bowls had been set around with warm water and flower petals releasing their scent along with the fluttering light of many candles. Yoshinori walked them over to the large bed. He rubbed hand down Kenji's arm feeling the young man tremble. Yoshinori pulled him close. Kenji melted into the kiss as Yoshinori sealed their mouth together. He offered his tongue for the gentle slide.

    Moist heat circled his mouth. Kenji sighed into Yoshinori's mouth. Gasping as he backed away. "Come here Iris Kouji, show me what he likes." Kouji stared at the patron in awe. Yoshinori could not deny the thought of seeing the two together had him aroused beyond measure. His feet moved on their own until he was standing beside them.

    "His neck is sensitive," Kouji explained placing his mouth on Kenji's neck. Yoshinori smiled seeing the nibbling kisses. That small pink tongue darted out licking along Kenji's neck. Kenji began to suck his own bottom lip moans escaping as Kouji pressed kisses to his neck.

    "Just like you," Yoshinori smirked he recalled the night he had taken Kouji. He had made sure to show the young man pleasure. He leaned back watching as the boys pressed kisses to each other. He thought of his night with Kouji in the back of his mind he had envisioned this exact scenario.

"What else does he like?" Yoshinori asked. With gentle hands he peeled the sash back of the white satin robe. "Do these like to be licked?" He asked flicking a finger over the peachy peaks. Kenji's face turned away as his cheeks bloomed with color.

"Yes," Kouji panted giving in to the surreal pleasure of the demands. With a groan he trailed his tongue down to the peak of the chest. Yoshinori followed suit latching on the left as Kouji sucked on the right.

"Oh... no...No no no," Kenji whimpered as his knees began to weaken.

"You mean, yes," Yoshinori grinned

pushing the robe all the way free of the lithe form. "Yes indeed." Yoshinori backed away sitting on the bed. "Make him ready for me," Yoshinori leaned back on his elbows watching as Kouji trailed his hands and his mouth over the slender body. Kenji could feel his face heating as his body responded to the caresses. "How does he like to be stroked?"

"We've only... I mean, once," Kouji looked away as he could not show Yoshinori what he wanted.

"Come here," Yoshinori patted the bed beside him. Kenji and Kouji walked over. Kenji sat beside Yoshinori with Kouji on his left. "When you kiss, I see things in an entirely new way. I am thoroughly aroused . "Why?" Yoshinori moved back on the bed until he was behind both boys. He stroked a hand through each of their hair, turning their faces to each other. "Why is this turning me on so much?" Yoshinori moved Kenji until he was kneeling on the bed with Kouji behind him.

Kouji placed kisses along the smooth,w arm neck. "It is... I don't know," Kouji panted. Kenji's head fell back baring his neck for more of his nibbling kisses. Yoshinori reached between the two until he could feel the hardness of Kouji. He stroked trailing his fingers in the leaking from the tip. "Mmm," Kouji groaned holding tight to Kenji.

"Show me how you touched him," Yoshinori purred as he moved behind Kouji. He moved his hips, rubbing against the firm bottom that had spent years on the soccer field. High and pert it sat, perfectly round and firm. "Lay back," Yoshinori pushed Kenji back on the bed. He stroked the thighs as they spread making sure that Kouji's hands followed after his own. Kouji saw the turgid length straining as it poured out liquid arousal. "Touch him for me."

"Kou-" Kenji panted as his needs escalated. Kenji gasped, feeling those slim fingers encircled him. Yoshinori grinned as he stroked up and squeezed. Kouji did the same. Yoshinori then stroked down. Kouji mirrored the move. Yoshinori took the foreskin down, tracing his finger over the exposed tip. "Oh... Kou," Kenji bit his lip as he feared the heightened level of his own body heat.

"How does he taste?" Yoshinori asked leaning down over the prone form. "Show me," Kouji did not hesitate. He placed his mouth over the erect member tasting the juices as they escaped. Kouji licked down then up again. Before he could go back down, Yoshinori pulled his head up sealing their lips. The glistening nectar coated their lips. Together they went down, licking and slurping over the writhing member of Kenji. "Let's loosen him. I want in him soon." Kouji nodded sucking a finger in his mouth. "Did you find it?"

"Find?" Kouji looked back at Yoshinori his brows drawn together as he wondered what the patron was asking him.

"It's okay, I did not find it the first time with you, we can find it together." Yoshinori promised with a grin. He reached over to the night stand finding the lubrication. He coated his fingers. "Just relax for me little Iris," Yoshinori whispered with a soft kiss on the tip. He kissed the thighs as he spread them. Kouji leaned up on the bed. He interlocked fingers with Kenji as Yoshinori pressed two fingers inside of him.

"Ah..." Kenji turned his face to Kouji. With his free hand, he pulled Kouji's face to his. "This is all just a dream." Kenji panted as Kouji sank down claiming his lips. Kouji reached down. As Yoshinori probed inside of Kenji, he stroked until he knew that

Kenji was on the verge of release. "Alright, now," Kenji panted wanting to feel the deep possession that he had felt in Kouji's arms. Yoshinori positioned himself. Kenji squeezed Kouji's hand as with a slow, wet thrust he was claimed.

Yoshinori began to move then. Feeling the deep plunge as he rocked inside of Kenji. He leaned back, "Come here Iris Kouji." Kouji sat up from where he had been kissing and licking Kenji's lips. "Bring your leg over." Yoshinori helped Kouji to straddle Kenji's hips. Yoshinori stroked Kenji with his lubricated hands spreading the sweet smelling mixture over the hardness. He then positioned him. "Relax and slide down." Yoshinori coached making sure that Kenji entered with a smooth thrust.

Yoshinori smiled as he parted Kouji's cheeks watching as the full length breached him over and over again. Kouji gasped, panting as his body accepted the sensual invasion. Yoshinori held on to Kenji's hips. He felt his own end near as he pushed into the newest flower. That tight sheath held him. Kenji thrashed upon the bed raising his hips taking Yoshinori in as he was claiming Kouji.

The twins panted, moaning as their bodies gave in to their youth. Yoshinori gasped feeling the tight, throbbing climax. He held the hips still as he lost himself to the pleasure surrounding him. With a few deft movements, Kouji spilled coating Kenji's stomach with his release.

"If this is a dream," Yoshinori smiled kissing each in turn. "Then it is a good one. Enjoy it while it lasts, the real world is a nightmare." Yoshinori leaned back in the bed. "Humans are the worst monsters you will ever come across. Best to remain a flower in a dream than the alternative." Yoshinori stood from the bed. "Both of you take a bath. Welcome to the Garden." Kenji crawled over to Kouji's side. He pulled the blanket up around them against the chill in the room. Yoshinori left the room without a backward glance, shutting the door softly behind him.

Chapter 9

Goji stood outside the door to the Iris suite. With Seitaro left sleeping in his bed, this was the best time for him to check on the newest flowers. How Mochizuki could rationalize what he had done, Goji would never understand. Was it not the role of family to make sure that the young never ended up in places like this? Goji rang the bell recalling a moment in his youth when he had run to a door banging on it until his knuckles bled. Now his hands were so soft he could not fathom knocking on a door without bruising.

When he received no answer Goji sighed. Should he come back later? Goji was just turning to leave when the door of the suite opened. "Kouji?" Goji asked seeing the disheveled young man standing in the door way.

"I am Kenji," Kenji said with a smile. In the dim light he knew that the Orchid could not see his eyes clearly. There was not any other way to tell he and Kouji apart really.

"Well, good morning to you then, Kenji" Goji said with a smile. "You look well loved." Goji said his smile still in place. He glanced over the bruises along Kenji's neck. His lips were swollen with a deeper red tint. "Where is Kouji?"

"In the bath, I was on my way in with him," Kenji explained. He stood back allowing Goji into the room. Goji walked across the plush carpet into the bathing chamber where Kouji leaned back against the soft terry cloth pillows. Kenji sighed, dropped his robe and stepped into the water. Goji smiled finding this youngest twin amusing.

"I would offer to join you, yet I am sure that Seitaro will be up soon." Goji grinned He trailed his fingers in the water. "Yoshinori called this morning and suggested I check on you." Goji stood to his feet looking down at the twins as they reposed in the bathing area. What Yoshinori had actually said was that he should make sure that the boys were not wallowing in grief, or regret. Kouji looked up with a soft smile on his face. Goji gasped as the smile did not reach his eyes.

"Goji," Kouji said after a moment. "How old are you?"

Goji smiled down at Kouji. "I am twenty three years old. I will have worked off my debt to the Genzo group in another year." Goji sighed. "I can't wait."

"The dream will be over then," Kenji said dipping his entire head into the water as his eyes clouded over. He was not crying. He affirmed as he sat up shaking his head until water splashed over Kouji and Goji. He was not sad, he was living in a dream.

**~~

Yoshinori walked the long halls of the office building with a portfolio under his arm. He knew that the main secretary would not want to let him through, yet he had to catch Mochizuki before he left on his next business trip. He had not lied when he told the boys that he was not often in town. In that respect, they would be better off in the Garden.

"Yoshinori-San," Mochizuki stood up from his desk with his hand outstretched.

He had his most congenial smile in place as he greeted the high powered lawyer. Yoshinori bowed instead with his hands clasped in order to show the signet ring with the symbol of the Osaka Garden that graced his right hand. The flowering vine around a metal gate winked in the early morning sun. Mochizuki nodded his head to acknowledge that Yoshinori was here to see him on official Garden business.

"Come in, shut the door. It is quite alright Itsuzu," Mochizuki waved his secretary away. Mochizuki sat behind his desk extending a hand for Yoshinori to sit opposite him at the large marble monstrosity.

"I bid you a good morning," Yoshinori smiled then took a seat. "I have some paper work for you to look over. It will be a great benefit to all involved. You will find it to be quite a lucrative deal in the end." Yoshinori held over his portfolio.

"This is the paper work necessary to buy out your brother's business. I will be the main shareholder at a tidy little profit for you." Mochizuki gasped as he looked into the files.

"No," Mochizuki sat the file down. "I promised that the business would remain in the family."

"And so it shall," Yoshinori promised. "Please continue to read the documents. The business will be signed over to the boys when their terms in the Garden have ended."

"*Their* terms?" Mochizuki gasped. Had they already found out about his indiscretion? *They*? He had only had one. He had planned to give Kenji time before he took him. When he returned next month he would treat himself to the boy's first time, then release them to the populace of the Garden.

"Both young men are now Iris Flowers of the Osaka Garden. They signed on for a promise that they would regain their business at the end of their term and we would destroy all records of their habitation. Last night Kenji was blossomed good and proper, Kouji witnessed."

"Who?" Mochizuki gripped the arms of his chair. "Who touched my..."

"Brother's children..." Yoshinori said when he saw that Mochizuki was getting louder. "Your nephews? Your family?" Yoshinori ground the words out. "This silence pact goes both ways. Either you agree, or the world of your constituents will find out just how depraved you really are."

Mochizuki leaned back in his chair. He held on to the portfolio. His hands shaking a bit as he recalled the pleasure that he had derived from the moment he had been with Kouji. Knowing the boy had capitulated under duress had made it all the more sweet. The way he had bit down on his pillow to hide his screams.

Mochizuki had gone harder hoping to make him break, make him cry out. What would his constituents think if they found out? Would Yoshinori actually do it though? If he did go public with the information, wouldn't his own involvement in the garden be exposed? "I know exactly what you are thinking," Yoshinori said with a grin. "If you could look behind the bill of sale, you will see documentation from the other patrons all ready to buy you out of your shares in the Garden."

"How dare you!" Mochizuki's face went florid as the file was launched across the office. "My family was a member of the original group that started the Garden, here in Osaka, in Edo and the Tokyo Garden are all thanks to my clan."

"And somewhere along the way your cruelty has exceeded the tolerance of the gentle flowers." Yoshinori stood to his feet. "They are bred for a gentle touch. They are made for titillation and pleasure, not sadomasochism. They are trained to be fragrant and sensual." Yoshinori kept his voice as soft as he could. He was careful as he gathered up the files and paper work. "We understand if you have a problem, that is why the Inu Koro inn exists. Indulge yourself there, they expect it." Yoshinori sighed. He had never been to the Inn and found the premise disgusting yet if that is what it took to get the twins freedom, so be it.

Mochizuki frowned as he looked at the forms that Yoshinori had prepared. "If I sign this, I get the next bud. I don't care who it is. I want the next blossoming bud."

"That would be Kira, and she is already scheduled for Ichi," Yoshinori said glad that the young girl he had found in his Aunt's tea house was safe. He had vowed never to touch her as she was his third cousin, yet he could not allow her to continue to be mistreated. While he would not take her, he would not allow her to be deflowered by Mochizuki.

"The next one then." Mochizuki demanded. "I don't care who it is, male, female, the next budding flower is mine!"

"Fine!" Yoshinori surged to the edge of the desk. The motion to hand over his pen snapped it in half. Yoshinori ran a hand through his hair before he reached into his pocket for another pen. "Just sign the damn paper."

Mochizuki affixed his name to the bottom of the forms. He then went through initialing several spots, then signing off on the sale of the Shipping and trade business that his brother had once owned. "It was you, wasn't it?" Mochizuki snarled as Yoshinori gathered up the papers. "You are the one who had Kenji. I was waiting for him to come to terms with it, to come to me himself." Mochizuki sighed, after a moment. "I meant well."

How much bile could one person swallow in such a short visit? Yoshinori had ceased to count as he thought of Mochizuki with his hands on Kouji and Kenji. He only hoped the patron was shamed enough that he did not go for the boys again. If he thought that was good intentions... Whatever. As long as he had signed the forms.

"I know," Yoshinori went to the door. "In the beginning, we all did." Yoshinori gathered up his collar on his shirt against the light drizzle that had been starting outside. "The road to hell is paved with good intentions." Yoshinori muttered. Gripping his portfolio, he forged out into the gathering storm.

**~~

"That's beautiful," Kouji stood behind Kenji as he sat his paintbrush down. He stared at the red canvas with flames painted as if it were water washing upon the beach. Rubies poured forth from the mouth of the whales as they soared against a golden sky. "What will you name it?"

"It is called Yume no akumu." Kenji wiped his hands on a rag. The world of flames reminded Kouji of hell, yet the watery theme was that of a calm serenity often found in his dreams of the ocean. He had discussed the dreams with Kenji when they were thinking of trying out for the swim team as opposed to basketball or soccer.

"I wonder how the team is doing," Kouji mused. He thought that the boys on the team would be in training as they prepared for the finals. "Time seems to stop here, it make no sense. Our birthday is coming around again."

"Is it?" Kenji gathered up his brushes and supplies. "Hmm." He shrugged his shoulders. Kouji looked after his brother with a sigh as he carried his brushes into their bathing chamber. Kouji sat on the lounge listening to the soft sounds of water swishing. He held the note in his hand waiting for Kenji to come back out.

"Katsu sent a note around," Kouji explained the note in his hand. "He will be here tomorrow to see us. He will have dinner with us." Kouji handed his brother the notes. "For some reason we are instructed not to bathe before."

"Katsu, he likes to bathe with the flowers before taking them," Kenji explained as he thought about a previous conversation that he had with Goji about each of the flowers and the patrons. "A lot of his fun starts in the bathtub. Does he want us both?"

"Yes," Kouji affirmed the request for them both with a soft sigh. Kenji nodded his head as he set his brushes up to dry. "Come on, lets have a go with that new computer simulation that I got. It's the closest to soccer that either of us will get in a while."

"Oh, yes," Kenji laughed thinking of all the hard won calluses that had vanished after months of inactivity and sugar scrubs. "In the morning if we are not too sore, we should go to the gym. We are allowed the treadmill and exercise bike so long as we do not become too muscular."

Kouji looked over at his brother with a soft smile on his face. Kenji frowned gazing at Kouji hoping to ascertain what he was wanting. The glisten in his eyes vanished under the fluttering of his spiked lashes. "Do you ever wish that we were in the car with mom and dad?"

Kenji smiled back offering a slow shake of his head. "As long as we are alive," with a soft rustle of pale peach and yellow satin, Kenji was at Kouji's side. "There is hope to improve life. I mean it is not all bad. We are together, closer than we have ever been and if you are honest, you will admit that it does feels good. As long as Uncle does not visit, we will be fine. I don't even mind if you take me. I mean it's just a dream right?"

"Yeah," Kouji fought back a sniffle. "This is just a dream. This place does not actually exist. It is a throwback to the times of the Meiji era. We are trapped here, just like the previous flowers lost in the Chaos of the war with the Shogunate."

"Yes, just like petals on the wind."

Kenji wrapped his arms around Kouji marveling that where his outer garment was peach, Kouji's was yellow and where his was yellow, Kouji's was peach. The Obi holding the silken cloth loose to their slender frames were various shades of white, blue and gray. "I will always love you Kou-Chan. We will get through this." Kouji held his brother tight burying his face in his Iris scented neck. They were thus, holding each other when the door opened. Both boys turned to face their patron. Kouji blinked at the flash of the camera.

"Genzo-Sama," Kenji smiled keeping his brother in his arms.

"It is our pleasure to entertain you," Kenji and Kouji said in unison.

Owari

Extra

Kouji dragged a brush through his hair. When he played soccer, he always made sure to keep it just below his ears. Kept the hair from suffocating him. Kenji was the same. Now their hair fell to just below their shoulder's. Soft, iris scented strands of honey settled after the vigorous brushing. "I'm surprised you are not bald yet." Kenji took the brush to his own hair.

"Sorry, I am not as delicate as your fine self." Kouji glanced at the mirror. He saw the earrings in his ears. Recent acquisitions at the whim of Katsu who figured having emeralds would highlight their eyes. " Did you disinfect your ears today? Don't want them infected."

"Yes 'big brother'," Kenji showed the cotton swabs along with the solution from the jeweler. "Now who is coming to see us today? I did not think that we had a patron visiting." Kenji looked over their notes on the desk. "Not until this weekend, we are accompanying the Genzo brothers to the opera."

"Yes," Kouji sighed recalling the instructions to dress feminine and not speak. He had already arranged for Sakura to come help them with their make up. "No one will be able to recognize us not that they would anyway." Kouji sighed running his hand through his hair.

The two boys from the newspaper clipping posing with the soccer trophy were no more. Gone was the short hair and athletic physic. Gone were the uniforms and sneakers, the sweats and bruises. In their place were fragrant, sensual creatures. Kenji opened his mouth to ask again who was coming when the chime sounded on the door. He gasped to see Harumi from the Rose suite enter.

"Hello," Harumi, her pink white and red ensemble floating like silk into the common area. "Tea?" Kenji backed away allowing her into their suite. Kenji looked away feeling his cheeks heat as she stared at him. "You are adorable. You have been blossomed for about five months now, and Kouji tells me that you still have never even kissed a girl."

"Kou!," Kenji turned his glare to his twin. "When you visit other patrons and flowers leave me out of it."

"I'm just trying to help you out." Kouji ran a hand over Kenji's side. "I mean, don't you want to kiss a girl?"

"This girl wants to kiss you." Harumi sidled over to Kenji.

"Yoshinori had Kouji and I last week. It was beautiful. Are your lips as soft?"

"Softer," Kouji told her. "He actually uses that exfoliating stuff they send us." Kouji chuckled. "Her breasts feel like dreams and miracles. You should touch one. Or both." Kouji pressed into Kenji's back. With a soft touch he brought Kenji's hand to his lips. "They taste even better. Come on, lets have some fun." Kenji could feel his face heating as he followed Kouji and Harumi to his room.

Kenji sat on his bed staring up at Kouji and Harumi where they stood before him. "Do you want to kiss me?" Harumi asked sitting at his side.

"He does," Kouji answered for Kenji simply swallowed the surfeit of moisture in his mouth. Kenji licked his lips, leaving them glistening. He leaned forward, his hand resting on Harumi's shoulder. The first touch of her lips brought a sigh. Harumi opened for him, her mouth drinking in the tentative tongue that tasted her. Kouji moved Kenji's hand from her shoulder until he was cupping the nubile breasts.

Kouji reached between them. He

untied the obi allowing the loose garment to fall. The shining material slithered to the floor forgotten as Kenji stared moved his lips from Harumi's to stare down at the body bared to his hungry eyes. Harumi giggled, "It is good that our clothes are meant to fall away with little provocation." Kenji gasped as Harumi pulled the sash holding his own robe closed. "You are truly beautiful." Harumi's whispered words brought more color to Kenji's face.

"Touch her," Kouji said soft in Kenji's ear. He placed a kiss on the delicate lobe trailing his tongue down the side of Kenji's neck. Kenji allowed his hand to be moved again this time his smooth fingers teasing the tips of the peach hued peak of Harumi's left breast. Kenji sighed filling his palm with the plump flesh.

Harumi arched into the gentle touch. "Taste me," Harumi brought her hands to the sides of Kenji's head bringing his mouth down to hers again. That sweet tongue trailed inside while Kouji moved to the other side of her. He cupped her breasts in both hands pinching the peaks until they stood at attention. Harumi leaned her head back resting against Kouji a soft moan leaving her lips. Kenji's mouth traveled her neck to her collar bone until he was staring at the lovely pert tips. Kenji swallowed before he placed his mouth to the swollen nipple. Harumi moaned moving her deep brown hair aside so that Kouji could continue to kiss and lick her neck. "Mmm, you boys do overwhelm a girl."

"Delicious," Kenji sighed sucking deep drawing the taut nipple into his mouth. Kouji moved around to the front of Harumi so that he could tongue the right as Kenji laved the left. Harumi burrowed her fingers in their soft hair holding them close. A hand, who's she could not tell, stroked her inner thighs causing her legs to shift releasing the rose scented evidence of her arousal.

"She's wet," Kouji said to Kenji pushing his finger past the soft folds stroking until Harumi raised her hips to meet his hand. "Taste," Kenji opened his mouth to suck Kouji's finger as it pressed past his lips. "You should try it fresh."

"Yes," Harumi shifted until she was prone on the bed. The rest of her ensemble slithered from her shoulders falling to the bed then pooling onto the floor. "Taste me." Kenji stared at the soft feminine folds glistening with arousal.

"Be gentle, use your tongue." Kouji encouraged once again trailing a finger through her inner thigh. "Only nibble softly." Kenji slowly made his way down to Harumis womanhood tasting it only slightly. He felt her twitch but pleasantly. At that moment instinct took over and Kenji flicked his tongue quickly over her mound until he felt her whole body vibrate and her legs tightened around him.

Her moans spurred him to further action. Licking her deep within. He could not recall tasting anything so sublime. Was this the scent of a woman crawling in his head making him so aroused? "Now its my turn." Harumi smiled as she shifted to face to face with Kenji. Gently nibbled on his ear as she led his hands back to her breasts. Tasting his mouth again, her hands meandered down to his manhood.

"Did you forget I was here?" Kouji laughed as he pushed them both back onto the bed grabbing Kenji's face slightly. Kenji breathed in, relaxing into the feel of the pair of hands touching him. Harumi brought a slender leg over straddling Kenji. "It is time," Kouji whispered with a soft kiss to Kenji's ear. He stroked, once, twice before he moved the excited head against the soft, wet folds of womanhood

"Oh... My... Mmmm" Kenji gasped sinking into the tight, heat. Harumi moaned sinking down wiggling her hips taking the young man inside of herself.

"Just hold on," Kouji placed his brother's hands on Harumi's hips. "She knows how to ride."

"You feel so good inside," Kenji gasped raising his hips thrusting into the pliant body on top of him. Harumi ceased her cries long enough to lean down until their mouths met. Kenji returned the kiss with a sigh. His body was overheating he knew it, but there was nothing he could do about it.

"You have a great size to you, not too thick, but long enough to reach deep." Harumi wriggled breathing in heavy pants as her body convulsed around him. She felt hands on her breasts. Harumi leaned her head back. Turning to the side she opened her mouth sucking in his tongue.

Kouji pushed Kenji's legs up until they braced Harumi's back. "Relax a bit." Kouji held up two fingers covered in lubrication. "I am all riled up." Kenji gasped feeling the fingers probing. He relaxed as Kouji eased inside of him.

"Wait..." Kenji panted. "I'm going to."

"It's alright," Harumi groaned riding the waves of her own climax. "We are given birth control every morning with breakfast. Go ahead."

Kouji grinned thrusting deep. "He's going."Kenji tried, he did, yet his body grew taut. He gripped Harumi's hips pushing up into her he came in a flood or pure pleasure.

The three of them embraced and explored each other for what seemed like hours. Kouji lay beside them spent and satisfied and lay back as Kenji and Harumi, finished as well, nibbled soft at each others lips.

Kouji laughed of the sudden, "See? Aren't you glad that I told someone you hadn't even kissed a girl yet?"

Kenji then hit his 'older brother' with a pillow. "Shut up Kou-Chan." His pout was ruined by a yawn. Harumi left the boys sleeping, wrapped around each other.

The End

Tiffany Passmore Iris

Made in the USA
Middletown, DE
18 October 2025